BALLAD OF YACHIYO

BALLAD

OF

YACHIYO

PHILIP

KAN

GOTANDA

THEATRE
COMMUNICATIONS
GROUP

Ballad of Yachiyo *is published by Theatre Communications Group, Inc.,*
355 Lexington Ave., New York, NY 10017-0217.

The Ballad of Yachiyo *was commissioned by South Coast Repertory and Berkeley Repertory*
Theatre. It was developed during the author's residency at Berkeley Repertory Theatre, spon-
sored by the National Theatre Artist Residency Program, funded by The Pew Charitable
Trusts and administered by Theatre Communications Group. The Pew Chartiable Trusts
also have underwritten the publication of this book.

Gotanda, Philip Kan.
Ballad of Yachiyo / Philip Kan Gotanda.
ISBN 1-55936-122-0
1. Japanese Americans—Hawaii—History—20th century—Drama.
2. Girls—Hawaii—Drama.   I. Title.
PS3557.07934B34   1996
812'.54—dc20   96-35081
CIP

Cover photo courtesy of the author.

Book and cover design by Cynthia Krupat.

First Printing, February 1997

FOREWORD

UNSAID

It started with a slip of the tongue. A name my father let inadvertently drop during a casual, late-night conversation about his days growing up in Kauai. A sister, Yachiyo, whom I had never heard mentioned before in all the talk-story sessions with him. Yachiyo. No one wanted to talk about her. She was to be forgotten. Her name not spoken. And yet it was. Yachiyo. Maybe it was the unconscious urge on the part of my father to release the secret shame. Speak the name that had been left unsaid on his lips all these years.

I learned the barest of details. She was my father's eldest sister; she fell in love with a married man, got pregnant, and after walking home all night through canefields and red dirt, committed suicide by ingesting ant poison. The year was 1919.

I also acquired the only remaining photo of Yachiyo taken shortly before her death. And one more. Both gotten from my cousin Kiku in Waimea just before Hurricane Iniki erased all other traces of her in a swirl of wind and water. The other photo was of Yachiyo's funeral.

Something about Yachiyo's story got into my body, into my soul. I wanted to try and write her story. And so I did. Try. I tried for years to write her story. I put it aside several times, returning later only to be disappointed again in my attempts. I did several drafts from several different character viewpoints, deconstructed the linear narrative after an encounter with David Hockney and his photo collage technique, and even took a special trip to Kauai spending several days searching the Kekeha Japanese Cemetery for her headstone because my cousin Yukio told me it might still be there.

No matter what I did I couldn't conjure up who she was. What her voice was. I'd done my homework, read the oral histories, spent time with my relatives and kept her photo looking at me on my desk. This I would intermittently exchange with her funeral picture. Never together, only one at a time. It somehow seemed wrong to put her portrait next to the picture of her casket. The two together spoke to a betrayal of some kind that I found disturbing. I waited for her to speak to me, her voice to be heard, to come in my dreams and reveal the story to her nephew, the writer. Nothing.

In time, the intervals of abandonment grew longer. Her pictures were set aside with others of family. New and more urgent writing projects came to the fore and Yachiyo's name was left unspoken. Again.

Then, several years ago, my wife Diane had an operation. While she was recuperating, the doctors and nurses were nice enough to let me stay inside her room. I took out my computer and began to write. And over the next few days and nights, sitting next to my sleeping wife, in that environment of the hospital, I came up with the draft that eventually became the play.

It's not the true story, or even a story drawn from complete factual interpretation. It's just the story that came out, by accident, at a moment of non-expectation. A nephew's made-up tale to complete something incomplete in his own family's story.

I've always felt people's lives, no matter how brief, no matter how seemingly uneventful on the surface, make a kind of ripple in their historical time, sending into motion a series of connected disturbances, interrelated emotions and intentions that seed the universe, eventually branching out to become its fruit—never lost, never really seen, but always present.

Perhaps Yachiyo looked at her younger brother, my father, in a certain way. Said something, didn't say something, stroked his head, made him laugh. Perhaps they sat side by side at my grandfather's fish pond in Mana, touching the water's surface and sending into motion that ripple that led to him one day speaking her name to a son who wanted to remember. After so many years. So many years of being unsaid. Yachiyo. There, I've said it. Said it as my father finally said it. Yachiyo. After all these years of silence. After all these years of buried shame.

Philip Kan Gotanda
July 10, 1996
Coalinga, California

BALLAD OF YACHIYO

Ballad of Yachiyo premiered at Berkeley Repertory Theatre (Sharon Ott, Artistic Director) on November 8, 1995 and subsequently moved to South Coast Repertory (David Emmes, Producing Artistic Director; Martin Benson, Artistic Director) in January 1996. The production was directed by Sharon Ott. The set design was by Loy Arcenas; costumes were by Lydia Tanji; lighting was by Peter Maradudin; sound was by Stephen LeGrand; original music was by Dan Kuramoto; puppets were by Bruce Schwartz; the production stage manager was Julie Haber. The cast was as follows:

YACHIYO MATSUMOTO—*Sala Iwamatsu*
HIRO TAKAMURA—*Lane Nishikawa*
HISAO MATSUMOTO—*Sab Shimono*
TAKAYO MATSUMOTO—*Dian Kobayashi*
SUMIKO TAKAMURA—*Emily Kuroda*
WILLIE HIGA—*Greg Watanabe, Eric Steinberg*
OSUGI CHONG—*Annie Yee*

Acknowledgments

The author would like to thank the following people and organizations for their help in making the writing of *Ballad of Yachiyo* possible: Berkeley Repertory Theatre, David Emmes and Martin Benson, Diane Takei, Yukio and Masaye Gotanda, Raymond Arao, Fumi Murayama, Kiku Tanita, Sato and Kenkichi Matsuda, Stella Gotanda, Warren Nishimoto and Michiko Kodama-Nishimoto of the Center for Oral History at the University of Hawaii, Professor Franklin Odo, Professor Ronald Takaki, Tomomi Itakura, Theatre Communications Group, The Pew Charitable Trusts and the Wallace Alexander Gerbode Foundation. And very special thanks to Ms. Sharon Ott (for helping steward this project along).

CHARACTERS

YACHIYO MATSUMOTO

HIRO TAKAMURA

HISAO MATSUMOTO

TAKAYO MATSUMOTO

SUMIKO TAKAMURA

WILLIE HIGA

OSUGI CHONG

TIME

Around 1919

PLACE

Kauai, Hawaiian Islands

AUTHOR'S NOTE

All pieces try to say something, do something, leave the audience with something. This one for me was different. It wasn't about politics, the tyranny of our cultural mores, the tragic death of my blood relation, or even about constructing the perfect play, though all were important considerations.

Rather this one for me was all about tone. An emotional feeling that I felt in my body when I first heard her name and that stayed with my body all through the journey of making it, unmaking it, and making it again. A kind of beautiful sadness. That's all. That was it. Not an answer, not a political statement. Just that. A tone.

ACT ONE

Upstage: a large scrim for slide projections. We hear the haunting strains of a Japanese plantation working song with both traditional and contemporary accompaniment. Projections of sepia-toned period photos of Kauai life dissolve into each other giving a sense of the world—the cane field workers, a pottery, family life, etc. We end with a photo of the real-life Yachiyo. A series of shots moves in closer on the grainy, sepia-toned image of her face. It fills the screen. The actress playing Yachiyo moves in front of the slide, the image's large face superimposed on her body. As she moves downstage, the slide dissolves to super titles: KAUAI, 1919.

Yachiyo is simple in appearance, with an understated, subtle beauty. As she speaks, lights come up on Takamura. He mimes what Yachiyo describes.

YACHIYO: In front of him sits a mound of clay which he is squeezing into a tall cone, he pushes it down, then squeezes it into a tall cone again. This helps to even the consistency of the clay and makes it easier to work with. All during this he is pulling on the base of the wheel with his feet to keep it turning.

TAKAMURA *(Calling out)*: I need more clay, prepare more clay for me!

YACHIYO: He is making *yunomi*, teacups. Takamura-san does this by working the clay back into a tall cone and by fashioning a measured portion at the top into a ball. He's done this so many times he knows just the amount to use by the feel. Then by inserting the thumb of his right hand he makes a deep pocket, drawing the clay up to make the walls of the cup with the same thumb and middle finger. It's all done in one motion. Now he starts to use some tools. First, he inserts a flat spatulate tool to make sure the *yunomi* has a clean surface on the inside. Then, he takes a *tombo*, dragonfly, because of the way it looks—

TAKAMURA *(Looking up, interrupting gruffly)*: Yachiyo! Hurry up!

(Takamura fades to black. Silence.)

YACHIYO: Just before the sun breaks it gets very dark. Inky black and silent. As if all the light and sound has been sucked out of the air. The wind dies, night birds stop singing and everything seems to be suspended. Waiting. This is my favorite time of day. It's so dark that the boundary between the night and my body blurs and I begin to come undone, as if I am a child again, my Mama's hands unbuttoning me, my Papa putting me to sleep. And I can drift, let go, releasing out into this night my sweat, my breath, my thirst. My shame...

(The sun begins to slowly rise. Upstage in half light we see the silhouettes of Papa and Mama stirring from sleep.)

PAPA: Yachiyo? Yachiyo?
MAMA: What is it Papa?
PAPA: Yachiyo, is that you? Yachiyo?

(Morning light begins to break the horizon. Yachiyo turns away from Papa and Mama as they fade to black.)

YACHIYO: It is a beautiful morning. The night was filled with many dreams and when I woke up, I was happy. I cannot remember any of them, the dreams, and yet I have this silly smile on my face. (*Picking up a worn leather suitcase and moving across the stage*) I was born on the island of Kauai. On the leeward side just beyond Camp Mana in an area called Saki-Mana. It's the dry side of the island. The soil is reddish in color and when you walk barefoot in it you leave a trail of red prints wherever you go. (*Glancing back at her path*) Papa says you don't need to know where you came from. Mama says you do. (*Pause*) The year is 1919. I am sixteen years old. My name is Yachiyo Matsumoto...

(*Yachiyo, holding the suitcase, stands in front of a door held open by Hiro Takamura; he is fortyish, dark, intense. He is wearing a work apron covered in clay and drinking from a bottle of sake. Since this is Yachiyo's romanticized memory of their first meeting, Takamura's demeanor is very friendly.*)

TAKAMURA: What do you want?

YACHIYO: Yachiyo Matsumoto? My father wrote to you. My father was a good friend of your wife's father. She wrote back—

TAKAMURA: Ahh, you're the girl...

OKUSAN (*Off*): Who is it? Hiro? Is it *Otōsan*'s [father's] friend?

YACHIYO: I came by myself. My Papa could not come. He sent this along.

(*She offers a letter to Takamura which he does not take.*)

TAKAMURA (*Calling back to Okusan*): No. He didn't come. Just the girl. (*Stepping aside so Yachiyo can enter. Jokingly:*) Come in. Yeah, come right in. Eat our food. Here, drink my liquor.

(*He pushes the bottle towards Yachiyo. She moves away.*)

TAKAMURA (*Jokingly*): Please order me around. Tell me what to do. What would you like me to do? Huh? Little girl has a mouth, tell me what to do? Huh? Huh?

YACHIYO (*Flustered*): I want to thank you and your wife for taking me into your—

(*Takamura motions with his hand for her to stop and stumbles away, singing drunkenly. Yachiyo stares after the disappearing figure of Hiro Takamura. Sumiko Takamura, also called Okusan, appears. She is mid-fortyish, older than her husband.*)

OKUSAN: Hiro...

(*Okusan notices Yachiyo watching the drunken Takamura. Yachiyo becomes aware of Okusan and catches herself. Okusan takes Yachiyo's suitcase. Yachiyo glances back one last time at Takamura. Okusan notices, then exits. Lights come up on Yachiyo's boyfriend, Willie Higa, with a cane knife under his arm. He is Okinawan, nineteen years old, sturdily built with a deep tan. He is a worker. Yachiyo watches as Willie lights a match and begins to run the flame over the open blisters on his hands. Willie speaks with a pidgin accent.*)

WILLIE: Yachiyo.

YACHIYO: Willie. What are you doing?

WILLIE (*Trying to laugh, hide the pain*): Yamaguchi-san taught me this. See, it seals the blisters up so you can keep working out in the cane fields. Hey, you sit down out there, the Portuge *luna* hit you with his "black snake" whip, make you bleed more.

YACHIYO (*Noticing his pain*): Willie...

WILLIE: This way my blisters won't bleed. (*Beat*) I won't get blood on your dress like I did last time.

YACHIYO: You know how Mama and Papa get if they catch us together.

WILLIE: Tonight, by the pump house.

(Willie lets the flame burn him, waiting for a response.)

YACHIYO: I cannot. No.

(Yachiyo can't take it and blows out the flame.)

WILLIE: I'll be waiting.

(Lights come up on Yachiyo's father and mother, Hisao and Takayo Matsumoto. Papa is sewing, watching Mama.)

MAMA: Ryoichiro! Mitsuru! Where're the boys? The food's gonna be ready soon.

YACHIYO: I have five brothers and sisters. Mama lost two babies at childbirth. And last year we lost my sister Hatsuko to influenza. *(She brings to the table a bowl with a damp cloth over it)*

MAMA: That the *tofu* [bean curd] from Mr. Sato?

YACHIYO: Un-huh. The boy brought it all the way out here.

MAMA *(To Papa)*: Sato said he's willing to deliver. Trying to take away business from Hamada's store.

PAPA *(Looking under the cloth)*: It's all lumpy.

MAMA: He was willing to give us credit, Papa.

(Papa tastes it, makes a face.)

PAPA: *Mazui* [Lousy]...

YACHIYO *(Exiting)*: I'll go check the rice, it's almost done.

MAMA *(Remembering)*: *Ara*, did Mitsuru fill all the kerosene lamps?

YACHIYO *(Exiting)*: Ryoichiro did it for him.

PAPA *(To Yachiyo)*: Come here Yachiyo.

(Papa stops Yachiyo to see if the shirt he's making will fit her.)

MAMA: Now where're the younger kids? Yohei! Ichan! Shigeno!

YACHIYO: Out back Mama, with Mitsuru and Ryoichiro.

PAPA: You've grown, huh Yachiyo.

MAMA: Make the front bigger for her Papa. What are they doing out there?

YACHIYO *(Embarrassed at her comment)*: They're getting honey. To trade at the *Pake* [Chinaman] store for crack seed. *(To Papa)* You don't have to make the front *that* big.

MAMA: Where? Not the *kiabe* tree behind the horse stall again?

YACHIYO: They said the bees rebuilt the hive.

MAMA *(Hurriedly exiting to the back)*: Last time they tried to smoke out the bees, the bees went crazy, bit up the poor horse.

(Papa measures Yachiyo in silence. Slightly awkward but they enjoy each other's company.)

PAPA *(Kidding)*: Maybe I should do this full-time, huh? I'd be working then.

YACHIYO: Mama would like that.

PAPA *(Shrugging)*: Not good enough. Just good enough for when you were all kids. *(Measuring)* I know you don't like what I make for you anymore. Not stylish like out of those catalogues you look at.

YACHIYO: I don't mind Papa.

PAPA: You thought anymore about what Mama talked about.

MAMA *(Off)*: Put that fire out!

YACHIYO: Rice gonna burn, Papa.

(Yachiyo turns to leave. Papa watches her exit as Mama enters.)

MAMA: Ryoichiro, Mitsuru, you hear me! Come inside. Bring the kids in too. And move the horse out of there! Shigeno,

Ichan, Yohei—come around the side and wash your feet first! *(To Papa)* Did you ask her again? Papa?

PAPA *(Going back to sewing)*: You worry too much about what people think.

MAMA: You want people to think your daughter is some farm girl from the *inaka*—no refinement, not good enough?

PAPA: That's not what I mean.

MAMA: I'm not worried about what people think of me, Papa. I just want Yachiyo to find a good husband.

PAPA: So she needs to learn *Chanoyu*? Go all the way over there to learn Tea to find a good husband? She helps out here with the cooking, takes care of the little ones—

MAMA: What? You want her to end up with someone like that Okinawan kid? *(Sees the kids off to the side, entering)* Ah, ah, ah—I said wash your feet first, they're all dirty.

(Yachiyo enters with a pot of rice. Mama encourages Papa to speak to her.)

PAPA: Yachiyo?

(Yachiyo doesn't respond.)

MAMA: Papa's talking to you.

(Beat.)

PAPA: Do you want to go stay with those people in Waimea?

YACHIYO: I'm not sure...

MAMA: She doesn't know what's good for her. Sneaking around with that Willie Higa boy...

PAPA: You have to go live there. Move to Waimea. You understand? That far away you can't come home—

MAMA: You want to end up working twelve hours a day in the

mills, come home to a batch of crying babies, too tired to take care of them, let alone take care of your husband's needs at night, 'cause—

PAPA *(Overlapping)*: Mama...

MAMA: —that's the kind of life you're going to have if you don't listen to me and go—

PAPA: Mama! Let her speak. Yachiyo?

YACHIYO *(Aside)*: If I open my mouth a thousand *papio* minnows will come shooting out going every which way....So I don't say anything.

MAMA: Stubborn girl.

(Yachiyo runs off.)

Yachiyo.

(Pause.)

PAPA: Mama?

(No response.)

You shouldn't be so hard on her.

MAMA: I know Yachiyo. She wants things.

PAPA: So she looks through the catalogues all the time. That doesn't mean she—

MAMA *(Interrupting)*: Other things, Papa. Other things...

(Pause.)

I already wrote them. I wrote Old Man Takamura's daughter a letter.

PAPA: What?

MAMA: It's what's best for Yachiyo.

PAPA: Takayo!

MAMA: Besides, we can't afford to keep Yachiyo at home any-more. Not with the money we owe at Hamada's store and Yohei's medical bills—

PAPA: I can go over to the Knapper Plantation—see if they're hiring.

MAMA: They won't hire you and you know it.

PAPA: Then I'll go to the McDonald Plantation.

MAMA (*Shaking her head*): You can't quit working in the fields just because you're tired Papa—

PAPA: I didn't quit working, I passed out, Mama. I passed out.

(Pause.)

MAMA: Yachiyo can earn her own keep and learn a new trade at the same time.

PAPA: Old Man Takamura's daughter probably doesn't even re-member me.

MAMA: You saved the old man's life—they owe you.

PAPA (*Under his breath*): I didn't save his life.

MAMA: Coming over on the boat from Japan he was sick, coughing up blood—you said so yourself.

PAPA: Yeah, but—

MAMA: Now they can pay you back. And what's so terrible about learning Tea Ceremony. Your sisters did. A young girl should learn those things so she can meet a suitable young man.

PAPA: That's all crap. You don't need those kinds of things here. You have too much refinement here it makes you weak. People step all over you.

(Pause.)

You shouldn't have written them, Mama.

(Dim to darkness on Papa and Mama. Yachiyo appears.)

YACHIYO: I'm not stubborn. It's just the things I feel I can't talk about. Because I don't know what to call them yet.

(Osugi appears. Osugi is Yachiyo's age, Japanese with a Chinese stepfather. It is night. Full moon. Osugi and Yachiyo are high on a bluff overlooking the ocean. A kerosene lamp sits next to them. In the distance we hear music. Osugi wears a maid's outfit. During the scene they pass a bottle of champagne back and forth, drinking freely. Osugi speaks with a pidgin accent.)

OSUGI *(Looking out)*: Dat one's a pig! Okay, your turn—what's dat one?

YACHIYO: I can't tell, Osugi.

OSUGI: Da cloud's changing, hurry up...

YACHIYO *(Aside)*: Osugi is my best friend. She works at the McDonald house. I call her "head to mouth"—*atama kara kuchi e.* She thinks something, out it comes from her mouth. No in-between stops. I sometimes wish I could be more like her...

OSUGI: Hurry up!

YACHIYO: I don't know, what?

OSUGI: A horse, a horse, yeah?

YACHIYO: Oh yeah, yeah, a horse. *(Watching for a beat)* And it's running, running—so fast its body is stretching out...

OSUGI: Getting long like an eel now.

YACHIYO: An eel, yeah. Umm, wouldn't you like some *unagi* right now. The way Tabuchi-san cooks it over the hibachi.

OSUGI: Umm, da best, with some hot rice. *(Noticing)* Ooh look, look, dat's Mrs. McDonald's butt.

YACHIYO: Dat big. Your boss's *oshiri*'s dat big?

OSUGI: Hey, if you never move, your butt get big, too. Just sit dere and do like this... *(Starts to point in several directions)*

Osugi get dis, Osugi get dat. Get dis, get dat, all the time. She do like dat.

YACHIYO: You gonna get into trouble taking the champagne?

OSUGI *(Shaking her head)*: Good, huh? Da bubbles make your nose tickle.

YACHIYO: This some new kinda work, huh. Just drink and fool around.

OSUGI: Dey all drunk and dancing back there. Da other girls take care of everything. Hey, I get you a job here. Da other girl, Shimokawa, getting big, starting to show, dey fire her as soon as they know.

YACHIYO: My parents have other plans for me. I dunno yet.

OSUGI: When I got da job at McDonald's? Happiest day of my life. I don't have to work in da fields no more. And at night I get to see Pantat. Dat's it. Big smile on my face. I have everything. I can die now. *(Passing the bottle to Yachiyo)* How 'bout you? What's your happiest day?

(Yachiyo thinks for a beat while she sips.)

YACHIYO: When I took the picture of me. Dressed up in the kimono Mama had Papa's sisters send from Japan. Then, that day. 'Cause as we walk to Miyatake's photo shop, everybody stare. *"Bijin,"* they whisper, "Matsumoto-san's daughter is growing up to be a beauty." And when I look at Mama and Papa? They almost busting open they so proud.

OSUGI: Dat's it?

YACHIYO *(Nodding)*: Un-huh.

OSUGI: Dat's your happiest day?

YACHIYO *(Nodding)*: Un-huh.

OSUGI *(Shaking her head)*: Un-uh, dat's not your happiest day. Dat's *their* happiest day. You still waiting, Yachiyo, you still waiting. *(She gets up and drags Yachiyo with her)* Come on, come on, I show you how da rich *haoles* dance.

YACHIYO: You should get Pantat to dance with you.

OSUGI: Come on, don't be such an old fart.

(Music volume rises, an up-tempo song. It's a fun and lively rendition. Osugi and Yachiyo start to dance. Osugi has to guide Yachiyo, pushing her along. Soon, however, Yachiyo is enjoying herself.)

Drink break, drink break…

YACHIYO: No, no, come on Osugi, show me the slow one now. Show me the slow one…

(Osugi grabs the champagne bottle as Yachiyo pulls her back. Osugi pulls Yachiyo close. Music changes to a slow tempo.)

OSUGI: Like dis.

YACHIYO: Like dis?

OSUGI *(Drinking from the bottle)*: Yeah. Just like dis.

YACHIYO: So close, yeah? The boy's body pushed up close like dis?

OSUGI: *Haoles* dance nasty, yeah. You can feel the boy's *chimpo* and everything if he gets excited.

YACHIYO *(Stopping)*: That's enough.

OSUGI: What? You and Willie don't do dis kind of thing?

YACHIYO: I'm thirsty.

(Yachiyo takes the bottle and takes a big gulp.)

OSUGI: Pantat and me, all the time do dis kind of thing. Not dancing, but you know.

YACHIYO: We don't do that kind of thing.

OSUGI: How come—Willie's cute, yeah?

YACHIYO: That kind of thing get you into trouble, Osugi.

OSUGI: You so old-fashioned Yachiyo. Everybody does it some.

YACHIYO: Do that kind of thing you end up bringing shame to your family. Then you have nothing, no family, nothing. End up like that Shimokawa girl.

(During the following Yachiyo moves away to a watery pool of lights.)

OSUGI: Shimokawa, she's a stupid girl, go too far. Go so far, cannot come back. And now, she don't even have no boyfriend to take care of da baby. I've got Pantat. He always take care of me. Just like Willie. He always take care you Yachiyo. He dance good, too. Hey, maybe we have a double wedding, yeah. You and Willie, me and Pantat, at da Japanese *Kaikan*—all our families dere. And lots and lottsa flowers—we'll have beautiful white blossoms falling down around us, we'll drown in a sea of white flowers!

(Yachiyo moves down by the water. She kneels and looks at her reflection in the moving watery lights. Osugi fades to black.)

YACHIYO: The water, it's like a mirror. *(She stares for a beat)* My face. It's changing. Or maybe it's just the inside of me looking out that's changing. All I know is that sometimes I find myself staring at a stranger. Like when I look at my photograph. I don't recognize her. Who is she? *(She reaches out and touches the water's surface)* She thinks things, wants to do things. . . . I wonder what it's like to look at the world from the other side. Through her eyes.

(Yachiyo starts to move her face towards the water, then stops just at the surface. She pulls back. Lights dim to darkness, then come up on Okusan in her Japanese-style Tea Ceremony room. She has a large Japanese doll in her lap. A lamp sits off to the side casting the doll's moving shadow on the shoji screens behind her. We hear a variation on traditional Japanese instrumentation for Bunraku. *This scene should feel slightly eerie, skewed. Okusan holds the doll. She touches it, runs her hands along the fabric, its face. She then lifts it up and*

sets it in her lap. Okusan begins to manipulate it, the attention shifting from Okusan to the doll as it comes to life. It is as if Okusan were imbuing it with her spirit. The doll raises its hand to its face, tilts its head, wipes a tear from its face.... Okusan fades to black. Lights rise to full on Yachiyo. There are Pikake *flowers next to her. She is cutting up a Montgomery Ward catalogue and pasting cut-outs onto a paper. Willie enters. When Yachiyo sees Willie she looks around. She calls off.)*

Shigeno, keep an eye on Ichan and Yohei.

WILLIE: You want me to go?

YACHIYO *(Shaking her head)*: Mama's at church, Papa's sleeping.

(Willie notices what she's doing.)

WILLIE: You know dat catalogue, your parents don't mind? Cutting it up like dat?

YACHIYO: We got the new one already.

WILLIE: Monkey Ward one okay to do dat with I guess, the paper gives da butt a rash. But da Sears and Roebuck Catalogue. Dat one da kine. Ooh, so soft, everybody fights over dat one at my house. Can I look? I like dis hat, look good on your head, yeah. And dis winter coat Yachiyo. All da thick fur. *(Teasing)* You gonna wear dat thing when da big snow come here?

YACHIYO: Maybe. Someday.

WILLIE *(Picking up a cut-out picture)*: Whoa, dis dress... Yachiyo? You got something going on in dere no one can see on the outside—yeah. Look like some sexy *haole wahini* walking down da street.

(Yachiyo grabs the picture back.)

YACHIYO: It's just a game I play with Osugi. It doesn't mean anything. It's just something we do...

(Pause.)

WILLIE: Hey, I'll get you dat dress okay? Yachiyo? I'll buy it for you.

YACHIYO: You can't afford it. *(Pause)* This kind of dress no one can afford. Maybe only the Plantation boss's daughter. *(Pause)* You ever seen snow?

WILLIE: What?

YACHIYO: Snow? You ever seen it?

WILLIE *(Shaking his head)*: You?

YACHIYO: No. Almost everywhere else in the world it snows. Japan, Mainland. Even a little bit on the Big Island. But not here...

Pause.

WILLIE: I gotta go. A meeting at Yamaguchi-san's house. We planning some things.

YACHIYO: Willie.

WILLIE: Yamaguchi-san says the Union gotta stand up if it want to get noticed.

YACHIYO: You stand up, the boss gonna knock you down, you know that.

WILLIE: Then we stand up again. *(Starts to leave, hesitates)* You gonna do what your parents say? Your Mama's telling everybody you're gonna be this young woman, nose stuck up in the air. Too good for anybody around here maybe.

(Yachiyo is silent. He turns and leaves. Yachiyo picks up the Pikake *flowers.)*

YACHIYO: *Pikake.* I put it by my pillow at night. It makes me dream while I'm still awake.

(She inhales the scent of the flowers deeply, then looks at her

cut-out dress. One or two white flower petals begin to drift down around her. She stares at her cut-out picture. Lights come up on Hiro Takamura. He is drunk, holding a bottle. Lights on Yachiyo dim to half. She watches Takamura.)

TAKAMURA *(Teetering)*: I feel...I feel...nothing...

(He puts the bottle to his lips and attempts to drink. Finds to his disappointment, it's empty.)

...nothing. *(Looks at bottle. Examines it)* What makes this? *(Taps bottle)* Not the bottle but this... *(Runs his hand along the curve of the bottle's surface)* What allows it to be is the nothingness. The space around the curve is what allows this line to be, to be defined in what?...In the nothingness around it. And what holds it up? Why all the nothingness on the inside. In fact, look well. More nothingness than some-thingness is what it is... *(Spins the bottle on the ground)* In Hiroshima, we throw pots on the wheel going this way. But here, on the other side of the world... *(Spins bottle the opposite way)*...here they throw pots with the wheel going the opposite way. *(Muttering)* Nothingness. Too much nothingness... *(Gets up. Moving upstage he starts to urinate. He is in despair)* The world is backwards here. There is no order. No order. I should have never left. Masako... *(Calling out)* I should have stayed and married you, Masako! Who cares whether you're a whore! Who cares what anyone says!

(As he urinates, the stars come out. Takamura is overcome with the beauty as the whole stage is inundated in stars. He starts to laugh.)

As I piss, in my moment of despair, this.... You show me this. Are you trying to tell me something? *(Laughing)* I give up. You win! You win!...

(Lights suddenly change. Okusan is standing there. Yachiyo fades to black.)

OKUSAN: Hiro!

TAKAMURA *(Buttoning up, embarrassed)*: I had to urinate.

OKUSAN: Off the *lanai*?

TAKAMURA: If I have to piss, I have to piss, okay?

(Pause. Takamura goes to get a drink. Okusan watches him.)

OKUSAN: I'm going to have her come and stay with us. Papa's friend—his daughter?

TAKAMURA: You don't know who the hell they are. Then out of the blue you get this letter.

OKUSAN: I met him once. *Otōsan* used to talk about him all the time. He saved *Otōsan*'s life. It might be nice to have his daughter in the house. Since Father passed away…

TAKAMURA: I'm having enough trouble getting set up. The clay's all wrong here, way too sandy. There are no materials for the right glazes—and I have no idea if this damn *nobori-gama* is even going to fire right. Back in Japan you have experts for this kind of thing, kiln building. Even my father would go ask Kayama-san, the kiln expert. He'll tell you how to build a kiln—the angle of the incline, the draw—and all it costs is a few rice balls. But here, I don't know…

OKUSAN: It could be fun. Like having a younger sister. And she can help out. You always complain about not having enough—

TAKAMURA *(Interrupting)*: What, another worker like the last local I had to fire. These workers around here, all peasants—they have the aesthetic sense of cows.

OKUSAN: It's so quiet around here in the evenings. You always go out and leave me alone.

TAKAMURA: That was our agreement, right? After work I can

do whatever I damn well please. What? Your Old Man is not here anymore. We don't have to pretend. *(Pause. Softening)* Look, the pottery will work. I know how to make pots. Wait till the first big firing. You've been firing all night, the kiln's finally cooled down, you begin to tear open the bricks covering the door—

OKUSAN *(Interrupting)*: You said the kiln might not work.

TAKAMURA: I know, I know, I said that but—

OKUSAN: Matsumoto's daughter is coming. I have made up my mind, Hiro. She is coming to live with us.

TAKAMURA: Okay. Fine. You and your Old Man. "Do this, do that," like an *inu* [dog]. Okay, that's all right. But at night the dog is free to roam.

(Takamura exits. Okusan fades to black. Lights come up on Yachiyo and Papa playing Go.)

YACHIYO: Papa? The farthest away I've been is Kekaha.

PAPA: Are you scared?

YACHIYO: No. *(Pause)* Maybe this is our last game, huh?

MAMA *(Looking in)*: Yachiyo, go to bed. Shimasaki-san is coming by early to pick you up and I want you ready to go. He charges extra for that broken-down buggy if you make him wait. Put away the game Papa.

(Mama exits. Papa starts to put the game away but Yachiyo stops him. They look at each other for a beat, then continue to play for a while in silence.)

PAPA: Remember when I had all those silk worms. I had my family send them over from Japan. Do you remember that? I used to let you take them out and play with them? You remember?

YACHIYO: I remember Papa.

PAPA: I wouldn't let the boys touch them. I had to yell at Mit-

suru all the time. They were feeding them to the birds. Just
Yachiyo.

YACHIYO: You kept them in that shack next to the old bath-
house.

PAPA: You remember, huh? You were *chi-chai* [tiny], what, five
or six or something.

YACHIYO: I have to tell you something. You promise you won't
get mad, Papa?

PAPA: What?

YACHIYO: I was feeding them to the birds, too.

*(Papa stares for a beat. Then breaks into laughter. Yachiyo
joins in.)*

MAMA *(Off)*: Yachiyo, go to bed! Papa...

PAPA *(Lowering his voice)*: Everyone around here was laughing
at me, thought I was crazy. Thousands and thousands of
those silly silk worms, crawling all over the place. I thought
I was so smart, so smart. That's why we live way out here, so
I can have my big silk worm ranch. Everybody was going to
wear silk. Ship it to the Mainland. New York, San Francisco,
Chicago—hell, even ship it back to Japan. Mama tried to
warn me. *(Beat)* "Crazy"....Maybe they were right.

YACHIYO: It was a good idea, Papa. It was a good idea.

PAPA *(Shrugging)*: Good idea, but...

(Silence.)

Yachiyo? You sure you want to go?

(No response.)

You don't have to go. You can stay at home, the whole family together.

YACHIYO: I'm all grown-up now, Papa.

(Papa is silent. He moves a piece.)

Would you show me one of your poems?

(Papa stops. Looks up.)

Mama said you used to write poems.

(Papa stares.)

PAPA: I don't have them any more. I burned them all. *(Beat)* Time to go to bed.

(Papa gets up, hesitant, then embraces Yachiyo. He turns to leave. Lights come up on Mama.)

MAMA: Listen to me. Flower arrangement and *koto*, too, if she is willing.
YACHIYO: Papa will be angry if he finds out.

(Papa is isolated in a pool of light.)

PAPA: You think you're all grown-up.
MAMA: You tell Mrs. Takamura that Papa wants her to teach you those things.
YACHIYO: Mama...
PAPA: Be careful. The world might think you are.

(Papa exits. Mama and Yachiyo dim to darkness. A tight pool of light comes up on Okusan with her doll. Music cue. As Okusan manipulates the doll, she begins to tell a story. A few white petals fall from above during this scene.)

OKUSAN: There once was a woman. She was young. She was beautiful. And she was in love with a man.

(Lights come up on a male doll, which is manipulated by the actress who plays Osugi.)

He was of a proud, noble family. He was very handsome. And the woman loved him deeply.

(Pause. The female doll looks towards the male doll, which turns away.)

She was very lonely...

(Okusan's doll slowly droops and becomes lifeless. Lights come up on Yachiyo by the water with Osugi. Osugi is upstage from Yachiyo listening.)

YACHIYO: When I was younger this older boy held me under the water as a joke. He was below me and had me by my foot. I was trying to get to the surface, I needed to breathe so badly I could feel my face about to explode. I remember seeing the sunlight entering from above. It was cutting through the water like long, transparent knives. I wanted them to cut me open, peel me out of my skin so whatever was me, whatever was wanting, needing to breathe so badly could get out. ... I go into the water. I go in but I don't put my face in. It still scares me. I don't dive deep beneath the surface. Not yet. *(Beat)* The farthest I've ever been is Kekaha, Osugi. I'm afraid.

OSUGI: Maybe you shouldn't go then.

(Willie appears in a separate pool of light.)

WILLIE: We're thinking about going on strike. We're talking to da Pilipinos, see if they join in with us. *(He turns to leave)*

YACHIYO: Willie...

(Willie stops.)

WILLIE: I thought you was gonna stay here. With me.

OSUGI: What about da double wedding? All da petals falling down around us?

(Willie and Osugi withdraw. As Yachiyo watches them leave, Papa, carrying a suitcase, and Mama enter. Papa, Mama and Yachiyo face each other in awkward silence.)

PAPA: *Ganbare yo.* Work hard.

(Pause.)

MAMA: Don't bring us any shame.

(Mama turns and leaves. Papa hands Yachiyo the suitcase. She turns and moves across the stage. Papa fades to black. Lights rise on Takamura holding the door open, a bottle of sake in his hand. In this rendition of their first meeting, Takamura appears as he really was.)

TAKAMURA: What do you want?

(Yachiyo glances back at her tracks, then back to Takamura.)

YACHIYO: Yachiyo Matsumoto? My father wrote to you. My father was a good friend of your wife's father. She wrote back—

TAKAMURA: Ahh, you're the girl...

OKUSAN *(Off)*: Who is it? Hiro? Is it *Otōsan*'s friend?

YACHIYO: I came by myself. My Papa could not come. He sent this along.

(She offers a letter to Takamura which he does not take.)

TAKAMURA *(Calling back to Okusan)*: No. He didn't come. Just

the girl. *(Stepping aside so Yachiyo can enter)* Come in.
Yeah, come right in. Eat our food. Here, drink my liquor.

*(He pushes the bottle in her face. She moves away. He gets
right in her face.)*

Please order me around. Tell me what to do. What would
you like me to do? Huh? Little girl has a mouth, tell me
what to do? Huh? Huh?

YACHIYO: I want to thank you and your wife for taking me into
your—

(Drunk, Takamura stumbles away singing. Okusan appears.)

OKUSAN: Hiro... *(Notices Yachiyo watching Takamura leave)*
Matsumoto-san's daughter? Yachiyo?

YACHIYO: Yes.

OKUSAN: Let me take that. *(Takes her suitcase)*

YACHIYO: My Papa could not come. He sent this. *(Offering the
letter)*

OKUSAN *(Taking it)*: Please, please, come in.

*(Yachiyo enters as Okusan stares in the direction of Taka-
mura's exit, then back at Yachiyo. Yachiyo takes in Okusan's
house, impressed at the surroundings. Okusan leads Yachiyo
to a meal already laid out. Two bowls of noodles with some
condiments. It's a simple meal but served in a very elegant
manner on small standing trays. The chopsticks are set on
small decorative stands. A pot of tea and two tea cups. Okusan directs Yachiyo to seat herself in front of a tray.)*

Please have a seat. I was expecting you.

*(Yachiyo eyes the bowls of steaming noodles as the long trip
has left her ravenous. She takes the invitation to sit as an invi-*

tation to help herself. She immediately digs in and begins to slurp down the noodles in a noisy and messy fashion.)

(Pouring the tea) Would you like something to eat?

(Yachiyo is embarrassed and stops. She notices how mannered Okusan's movements are and becomes intimidated. Okusan pushes the tea towards her. Yachiyo watches how Okusan drinks her tea and tries to imitate it.)

It's nothing special. Just something I threw together in case you were hungry. *Doozo*, please help yourself.

(Yachiyo begins once again to eat in a noisy, slurpy fashion; then she notices how Okusan is eating. She slows down, watching Okusan and trying to follow her appropriately mannered way of eating noodles. Yachiyo and Okusan fade to black. Lights come up on Papa and Mama. Papa's shirt is off and Mama is doing yaito *[moxa burning] on his back.)*

PAPA: Did you tell her about the poems?

(No response.)

Mama?

MAMA: She asked about them so I told her.

PAPA: She asked about them?

MAMA: She remembers us fighting about them all the time.

PAPA: I burned them all didn't I?

MAMA: I didn't tell you to burn them Papa.

PAPA: You're always saying, "You don't need to write poems here. It's a waste of time. You just need to know how to work." And now you want her to learn those things.

MAMA: Because she's interested in those—

PAPA: She's not interested in Tea, she's just doing it because you tell her to. *Atsui, atsui!* [It's hot!] You trying to set me on fire...

MAMA: *Yaito* is good for the muscle. I told you not to lift the crates, you should have waited for the boys. Always trying to prove yourself. The heat will help. Right here? *(Testing the muscle)*

PAPA: Yeah—ahhh...

(Mama puts another small ball of the salve on his back.)

If I just soak in the bath for a while, the hot water—

MAMA: Sit still Papa.

(They work a while in silence.)

PAPA: Mama?

MAMA: Hmm?

PAPA: What if she gets into trouble? Waimea is so far away.

MAMA: She's got a good head on her shoulders. You worry about her too much Papa.

PAPA: Old Man Takamura's daughter was always peculiar. And his son-in-law, the potter. We don't know anything about him.

MAMA *(Lighting a match)*: This is going to burn a little...

PAPA: I've heard rumors.

MAMA: He's not from around here. He's from Japan. A good family. His father is a famous artist I hear.

PAPA: *Atsui, atsui...*

MAMA: Be good for Yachiyo to be around those kind of people. She can learn something. Make a better life for herself.

(Papa reaches back and takes her hand.)

I still keep worrying Mama.

(Beat. Mama likes the hand-holding but it embarrasses her.)

MAMA *(Taking her hand away)*: Nothing bad's going to happen. I know.

(Lights come up on Yachiyo and Takamura. Continuation of the opening scene. Yachiyo assists Takamura who mimes the actions as Yachiyo describes them. All during this Takamura is barking commands. Lights come up on Willie reading a letter.)

YACHIYO: Then, he takes a *tombo*, dragonfly, because of the way it looks, to double-check the depth and width, but he hardly ever needs to make adjustments. He is very skilled, Willie.

(Willie takes the letter and burns it with a match.)

Finally he takes a piece of string attached to a small stick for the handle. He lays the string around the base of the cup—and as it wraps around he pulls, perfectly cutting the cup from the rest of the clump of clay.

(Willie exits.)

Takamura-san then lifts the cup off the clay, sets it aside and begins all over again. And through all of this the wheel never stops moving.

TAKAMURA *(Overlapping Yachiyo's last sentence)*: And through all of this the wheel never stops moving. *(He stops and wipes his hands)* I want everything set up for me by the time I get here, understand. First thing, light the stove and heat the water. The floors must be swept. And I want tea ready. And the clay must be prepared and ready for me to throw. Oh, and just before I arrive—I don't want it prepared too early. I get here at seven o'clock sharp every morning. Pour some of the hot water into the slip buckets next to my wheel—I don't like to dip my hands into cold slip. It stiffens the fingers. I will mix all the clays until I feel I can trust you, but you must wedge it for me. I need six wedged portions ready by the time I get here in the morning and six more by ten o'clock. Then after our noon meal and nap, six more. As I stated before, don't prepare them too soon or they dry out. Keep them covered with a damp cloth. I suppose you don't know how to wedge clay, do you? Watch. *(Demonstrates as he describes)* You work in a circular motion like this. Almost looks like a rough sea shell pattern. Then gradually work it into an elongated ball. What this does is to take out any inconsistencies in the clay's texture. It actually aligns the particles of sand in the clay. It's easier to work with. Now try it.

(Yachiyo attempts clumsily.)

No, no, not like that. Here, get out of the way. Now watch. *(He shows her again)* Now you try it again.

(Montage sequence: Takamura steps in and works the clay, then steps aside and Yachiyo steps in wearing a work apron and begins to mime shoveling with a shovel. Takamura, now wearing a hachi-maki *[headband], steps in and jerks the shovel from Yachiyo. Yachiyo steps away and begins to take her apron off as she continues to speak what she has written in her letter to Willie. She moves towards Okusan.)*

YACHIYO: I live in a room off of the work studio. They have given me a small oil heater but I hate to use it because it makes my hair and clothes stink—

TAKAMURA: No, no, this clay is mixed all wrong. Weren't you listening to me? It's way too sandy. Look at the texture. Feel it. You can't work it. It needs more of this red clay. The iron gives it a richer color in firing.

(Takamura and Yachiyo speak the following speeches simultaneously, their voices rising in volume as they attempt to be heard over each other.)

No! What the hell is wrong with you. I would send you back right now if my wife didn't want you here. A pot is only as good as the soul of the man who makes it. Within this domain where I make the pots it is your duty to see that the potter's soul is at peace. The *Ochawan* [Tea Ceremony teacups] I do on the hand wheel. And the "foot" is the key. The way the base is trimmed is the signature of the artist.

YACHIYO: I get up at six o'clock every morning. We have an *ocha* break at ten o'clock. I work till lunch, that's at twelve-thirty. Eat, nap, then start work again at two-thirty and work till sundown. Eat, dinner, bathe, then go to sleep.

(Yachiyo moves to Okusan who is in the middle of giving Yachiyo a Tea Ceremony lesson. She seats herself across from Okusan who is holding an Ochawan *teacup and examining its base.)*

OKUSAN *(Overlapping Takamura's last lines)*: The way the base is trimmed is the signature of the artist. If one is knowledgeable, one can recognize the artist merely by examining the foot of the pot. No, no, Yachiyo. Always with two hands. You are then less likely to drop the *Ochawan*. You are showing respect for it.

(Yachiyo seats herself and Okusan proceeds into the Tea Ceremony. Yachiyo is still visibly upset at Takamura's rough manner. Okusan places the cup in front of Yachiyo who picks it up and copies Okusan's movements. Okusan reaches in and corrects Yachiyo's turning of the Ochawan.*)*

Do you have a lover?

(Pause.)

YACHIYO *(Embarrassed)*: No.

OKUSAN: A girl as pretty as you could have one if she so desired.

(No response.)

How old are you?

YACHIYO: Almost seventeen.

(Yachiyo sips and makes a face. Okusan notices.)

OKUSAN: *Chanoyu* tea is very special. It has a bitterness. But you will grow to appreciate that quality. *(Beat)* He is not always so ill-tempered. Takamura-san. He can be very gentle if he wants to be. Please be understanding of him. He doesn't mean to treat you so harshly. He is just...unhappy. He is the eldest son of a well-known pottery family in Japan. But he gambled too much. So his father disowned him. Hiro decided to try his luck here. He met my father who was impressed with him. Father decided to set him up in business. We, of course met, and one thing led to another...

(Takamura enters.)

TAKAMURA *(Grabbing some things)*: I have to go out...

OKUSAN: Where are you going?

(Takamura ignores her.)

(Sternly) Hiro.

(Takamura stops.)

OKUSAN: You're not going into town, are you?

TAKAMURA: Seto's missing again. They need more men for the search party. He's probably passed out drunk somewhere, but you know his wife, she's half out of her mind with worry. He'll stagger home in a few days just like always, won't remember a thing. *(To Yachiyo)* Don't forget to check the stove in the shed. And turn the pots, they have to dry evenly or they'll crack. *(To Okusan)* Don't wait up for me.

(Takamura exits. Silence.)

OKUSAN: I am glad you are here. Sometimes it is lonely. We have no children.

(Okusan becomes lost in thought.)

YACHIYO *(Uncomfortable)*: Can we continue?
OKUSAN: Yes...

(Yachiyo lifts the Ochawan *and rotates it in a circular fashion two times, then sips. She wipes the lip of the cup and lowers it. Notices Okusan staring at her.)*

YACHIYO *(Embarrassed)*: Okusan...

(Okusan doesn't know what Yachiyo means.)

YACHIYO: Please. It makes me uncomfortable. You looking at me.
OKUSAN: I am sorry. I was just noticing how beautiful you are. When I was your age that is all I would think about.

(As she speaks, Okusan's doll is lit, manipulated by a person dressed in black. The female doll mirrors the movements described by Okusan. A few flower petals fall from above.)

Sometimes I would awaken at night, go to the mirror and stare at myself. In that world of shadows and dream, I would recreate my face. I would make my skin smooth and milky white like the inner shell of the abalone. My mouth like a freshly cut fig. And my eyes, the perfect arc of a wave just before it breaks. *(Beat)* But of course, when I awakened...

(The doll becomes lifeless and droops. Lights on the doll fade to black.)

Do you think he is handsome?

(Yachiyo doesn't understand.)

My husband. Takamura-san?

(Pause.)

YACHIYO *(Nodding uncomfortably)*: Yes.

(Okusan watches her. Okusan and Yachiyo fade to black. Lights rise on Takamura carrying a kerosene lamp, then come up on Yachiyo standing in front of the pond of lights. A musical sound cue evokes water. Yachiyo stares at the surface. She kneels and dips her hand in it, then lets the water drip back into the pond. We hear the sounds of water splashing. Yachiyo begins to disrobe to go swimming.)

TAKAMURA *(Calling)*: Seto! Seto!

(Sound cue of Buddhist funeral bell.)

They found Seto. I guess he tried to go swimming and was too drunk...

(Takamura sees Yachiyo.)

Masako...Masako...

(Takamura blows out lamp. Yachiyo is lit wading in a shimmering bluish pool of lights. She reaches out to the edges of the shadows and touches something. A distance away in a pool of light we see a naked man floating on his back. His legs and arms extend upwards, slowly wafting in the current. Yachiyo pulls back in terror.)

YACHIYO: Seto was naked. Floating there. His body is very muscular. You couldn't tell by just seeing him. He had come by Takamura's a couple of times trying to get work. Takamura-san would give him a drink then send him on his way. Seto was very forward. Once I caught him staring at me. At my breasts.... I never touched...

(She stares out at the body, her fascination overcoming her fear. She tentatively reaches out to touch the body. Blackout. Lights come up on Okusan and Takamura. Takamura is drinking sake and gesturing towards the tokkuri *and* guinomi *[sake bottle and cups] on the table.)*

TAKAMURA *(Sarcastically)*: This is wrong. This is all wrong. What's a good-looking piece of pottery like this *tokkuri* and *guinomi* doing here. This is not right.

(Okusan brings out a wooden bowl and places it on the table in front of Takamura.)

There, that's better. What really should be here is this...a crude wooden bowl. That's what belongs on this table. It's more in keeping with the aesthetic sense of the people here in this town. They don't want fine pottery in their everyday lives. They want wooden bowls that they can knock on the floor and not break when they're screwing their wives on the kitchen table. *(Knocks wooden bowls to the floor)* See. That's what peasants like. Not finite beauty with the inherent fragility of human nature... *(Drops the* tokkuri *from one hand, but saves it by catching it in the other below)*...but crude, pedestrian substitutions. At least in Japan the people could appreciate a good pot. The Japanese people here, like your father... *(Downs a cup of sake)*

OKUSAN: I won't tolerate you talking about my father that way. After all he has done for you—

TAKAMURA *(Interrupting)*: He was a petty merchant, who couldn't squeeze any more money out of the farmers who had wised up to him. Comes here and is lucky enough to figure out all the workers need things and starts a store—a shack, four walls and—

OKUSAN *(Interrupting)*: Which he was smart enough to make money with. And which he sold so you could start this pottery.

(Lights rise to half on Yachiyo standing with her eyes closed, as if sleeping in bed. She is tossing and turning.)

TAKAMURA: I should have never left Japan.

OKUSAN: This pottery where you said you could make great—

TAKAMURA *(Overlapping)*: The pottery will work, it will work!

OKUSAN: —works of art like your father back in Japan!!

(Yachiyo awakens with a start.)

TAKAMURA: I should have stayed in Japan. I should have stayed there—married Masako. To hell with what anyone says... *(Exits)*

OKUSAN: Where are you going? Hiro!

(Blackout on Okusan.)

YACHIYO *(Getting up)*: When I was a child I would hear sounds coming from my parents' room. I would wake up at night, hear them fighting. The walls were so thin, the sound would pass through them like dark, scary animals. In the blackness, I could feel their voices scurrying about my skin, and even though I would try to keep them out of me, my head buried beneath the covers, they would crawl inside my mind, these ugly, screaming animals.

(Lights rise to half on Papa and Mama making love. Soft moans.)

Sometimes I would hear moaning coming from their room. I used to think maybe Mama or Papa was having a bad dream and I would want to go in there. But something always stopped me. A feeling, inside...

(Papa and Mama fade to black.)

At night I still feel the dark scary animals scurrying around. I still feel—

(Lights come up on Willie, agitated.)

WILLIE: Da start of da strike got everyone nervous. Da Pilipino union went ahead first, so we join in, too. First time, Japanese and Pilipinos. Nobody knows what da company gonna do.

YACHIYO: It's so hot and humid, everybody's irritable. Takamura-san and Okusan had a violent fight. He's in a bad mood because the pots are cracking as they dry.

WILLIE: I think you should come home. I thought it over and it is not good for you to be dere. I talked to my cousin who lives dere in Waimea and dere is talk about da man and his wife.

(We hear thunder and rain.)

YACHIYO *(Listening)*: Thunderstorms. *(Beat)* At night I hear them yelling and screaming.

WILLIE: They've been married nine years and don't have no children. The wife's father had money but he was a drunken sot. And dey say the son-in-law's no better.

(Crashing thunder and the violent flash of lightning.)

YACHIYO: It scares me but it is quite beautiful. Why do they stay together?

WILLIE: No wonder—he's a *yoshi*. I can't see how any man would give up his own family name and take on his wife's and be some pussy-whipped male taking orders from her.

(Streaks of light.)

YACHIYO *(Holding out her hand to the lightning)*: I sometimes wonder if it will strike me...

WILLIE: I think it's a mistake to stay there. You should come home.

(He fades. The sound and lightning slowly subside. Distant rumbles and occasional flashes in the horizon. Lights rise to half on Takamura in front of a small bisque firing kiln. Small flames are coming out of it.)

YACHIYO: After Takamura trims the pots they must be completely dried—this has been hard because of the humidity—and then they are baked in a low fire...

(Flames die out. Lights come up full on Takamura opening the kiln and taking the pots out gingerly.)

Then they are ready to be glazed. *(Beat)* More and more I think that coming was a mistake. I miss Willie. I miss my family...

TAKAMURA *(Handing pots to Yachiyo)*: Here. Be careful. We still have to glaze them.

YACHIYO *(Noticing)*: The reddish color...

TAKAMURA: It's all the iron in the clay—be careful! They're fired just hard enough to take the glazes but they can still break easily.

(He is sweating profusely, water dripping from his brow. He reaches for some water but it's out. He's about to say something when Yachiyo, anticipating his needs, hands him a newly filled water container. He stares at her. She's uncomfortable.)

TAKAMURA: How long have you been here?

YACHIYO: Four months.

TAKAMURA: You like working with me?

YACHIYO: Yes.

TAKAMURA: No, you don't. You hate my guts.

YACHIYO *(Flustered)*: No, that's not true—

TAKAMURA: Lie to my wife. She's the one who needs it, not me. You do your work right and I don't give a shit what you think of me. Get the other pots ready for trimming. The ones I was throwing this morning—

YACHIYO: Why do you treat me like this? I'm trying so hard to do everything right. The way you want it. The studio has to be cleaned in just the right way. And the temperature in the studio—I open the window too much, I close the window too much, turn on the stove to make adjustments, then open the window again to compensate for the stove's heat—I'm trying, I'm trying Takamura-san, I'm trying!...

(Silence. Takamura stares at Yachiyo.)

TAKAMURA: Good. Good Yachiyo. Now try harder.

(Takamura goes back to work. Okusan enters with two dusters, rags tied to sticks. She hands one to Yachiyo.)

YACHIYO *(Trying to contain herself)*: Okusan and I dust the pots off, otherwise the dirt and soot will keep the glazes from sticking to the surface of the pots. Then we can apply the glaze. He is very nervous as this will be the first firing of his smaller test kiln. There have been many problems—because the pots can't dry thoroughly they have been breaking in the low bisque firing—

(Yachiyo drops a pot, shattering it.)

TAKAMURA *(Furious)*: Yachiyo! *(Beat, to Okusan)* Peasants and farmers, peasants and farmers...

(Takamura stomps off. Yachiyo, humiliated, goes to her room, takes out her suitcase and begins packing.)

YACHIYO: When he's not there, when I'm alone in my room, I always answer back, right to his face, I always have the answer. But when he's there, in front of me, scolding me, I shrink up, and become tongue-tied—he knows everything, I know nothing, I'm stupid. I hate it, I hate it.

(Okusan enters Yachiyo's room. Sees her open suitcase.)

OKUSAN: You can hear us fighting at night, can't you?

(Yachiyo hesitates, then returns to packing.)

YACHIYO: No.

OKUSAN: You hear us. These days he has no shame about showing the world how much contempt he has for me. In the beginning it was different. He liked me. He liked me very much. Then *Otōsan* died and he started to change. He became mean, insulting. Began to go out at night. *(Pause)* Hiro has a lover. A young Pilipino girl in town. She works at the taxi-dance place...

(Yachiyo stops packing. Silence.)

YACHIYO: Okusan? You asked me before if I had a...friend? Willie Higa. Back in Mana. He asked me to marry him.

OKUSAN: Do you love him?

YACHIYO: I don't know.

OKUSAN: He loves you?

YACHIYO: Yes.

OKUSAN: It is better to be loved. *(Beat)* This is for you. I want you to have it.

(Okusan takes out a wrapped package and hands it to Yachiyo, turns and exits. Yachiyo opens the gift to find a beautiful Tea Ceremony Ochawan. Yachiyo stares at it, then at her open suitcase. Yachiyo crosses to join Okusan. Lights dim, then rise on Papa and, separately, on Yachiyo and Okusan doing the Tea Ceremony with Yachiyo's new Ochawan. Yachiyo's able to do the drinking portion of the Ceremony smoothly, without a hitch. This goes on during Papa's following monologue.)

PAPA: Dear Yachiyo. Things are very busy at home. They are considering me for a job at the Knapper Plantation so I probably will start work soon. Mama will like that... *(Pause. Starts a new letter)* Dear Yachiyo. How is the Takamura family? Old Man Takamura, the father—whew! When he drank, you didn't want to be around. See, there are three types of drunks. Some people when they drink, they get sad. That's your Papa. Others, they get happy. But

Old Man Takamura, he was the third type. He got mean. It must have been hell for that daughter growing up in that house. He yelled, screamed obscenities, even beat up people. He liked my company. When he was sick on the boat coming over here I played Go with him. Read him some of my poetry. He liked my *tanka* verse.

One time Takamura got real drunk. This was after we got here and he was better. We were outside a local gambling house and he was picking another one of his fights. Only this time the old man was very drunk and the other man very big. So, like a fool, I tried to stop him. Old Man Takamura got furious. And he hit me. He hit me again and again. The other people had to pull him off. He almost killed me.

After that he started telling everyone that I saved his life coming over on the boat. He would say the same thing to me, then say if I ever needed a favor just to ask him. I guess after a while I started to believe it myself. I didn't save his life. He just felt guilty. *(Pause. Starts a new letter)*

Dear Yachiyo...

(Papa fades to black. Lights come up on Okusan with dolls. Yachiyo looks on. Okusan is recounting a tale. This is a continuation of the story Okusan started earlier. A few petals fall. Music cue.)

OKUSAN: There once was a woman. She was young. She was beautiful. And she was in love with a man. She was so lonely. Because though she loved him, he was not able to return the love. But she already carried his love within and could not release it. It grew inside her soul until she was filled with inconsolable grief. No one could help her, no one could save her. And in a fit of this sadness, the woman, young and beautiful, threw herself into the fire and perished, her ashes floating upward like a swarm of dark insects...

(Lighting change. Silence.)

OKUSAN: What did you think of the story?
YACHIYO: I don't know...
OKUSAN: You didn't like it?

(Yachiyo is silent.)

Yachiyo?
YACHIYO: Why do you like it?
OKUSAN: It's a very famous story. Based on a true incident. It's very beautiful. You don't think so?
YACHIYO: Yes, but...
OKUSAN: Yachiyo?
YACHIYO: Why did she have to kill herself?
OKUSAN: In order to preserve her family's honor. To save face for herself and her parents. Because there was nothing else for her to do. A beautiful death. You wouldn't?
YACHIYO: No. She should have figured something out. Gone on living.

(Okusan stares at her, then begins to laugh.)

What did I do?

(Silence.)

OKUSAN: Sometimes. When I'm alone, I visit my dolls. Play with them. Make them move. An arm this way. A head tilted this way. And after a while, the doll becomes me. It's my arm, it's my head. And I make up stories. About her. About me... *(Embarrassed)* I like you Yachiyo. I can talk to you. You can be my friend. My only friend, okay? Okay Yachiyo?
YACHIYO: Okay...

(Okusan exits. Yachiyo pauses for a moment, staring at the doll. She picks it up and begins to manipulate it while speaking the following lines. The dolls come alive.)

There once was a woman. She was young. She was beautiful. And she was in love with a man.

(The male doll, now lit, and the female doll begin to embrace. This is too much for Yachiyo and she turns away, moving to the pool of water. She's having her period and takes out a blood-soaked cloth from between her legs. She puts it into the river and begins to clean it. We see the growing red color as it spreads. As she does this, Osugi is lit and speaks.)

OSUGI *(Working)*: Dey finally let da Shimokawa girl go. She was pretty big. I was walking her home when dese workers from da plantation called her a prostitute and asked her to go in da bushes with dem. Everybody talking, whispering behind her back—she won't go out of da house anymore. And da mother is so ashamed she won't go out either so da little sisters have to do da shopping and everything. I don't let Pantat touch me dat way no more. Not till we get married. Dat kind of shame…

(Osugi fades to black. Takamura staggers along drunk, holding a sake bottle. Big moon in the night sky. Yachiyo hides and watches Takamura, who stands at the water's edge and talks to the night.)

TAKAMURA: My soul…my soul, an empty bladder, shriveled up with no song. No song. It used to be such a glorious roar. Explosive and deliciously indiscriminate. It needed so much, it wanted all the time. Days and nights on end of abandoned revelry—in drunken stupor, my cock in my hand waving it at any woman who would pay attention. But always it was about the pursuit of that mysterious thing. Yes, "thing," because I can't even name it, yet I can always sense its presence. Just beyond my grasp, just beyond the pale.

(Seto's naked body, upstage, is brought up in half light, floating. Lights rise to full on Yachiyo turning to look back at Seto's body. For a moment, Takamura stares at Yachiyo.)

Masako knew, Masako could understand...

YACHIYO: Once I caught him staring at me, at my breasts...

TAKAMURA *(Looking at his hands)*: Imperfect. *(Looking at the bottle's curve)* Perfect. *(Pause)* You give me the mind to imagine it, see it. And yet I cannot create the picture inside my head. Imperfect, perfect. My father's blood pushing through me, feeding me with his seed. And still...

YACHIYO *(Looking at Seto's floating body)*: I never touched a dead person before. I think you have to live life now. Because tomorrow you might be dead.

(Yachiyo turns to Takamura and slowly reaches out to touch him.)

TAKAMURA: Nothing, nothing, nothingness...

(Dim to darkness.)

ACT TWO

Lights come up on Yachiyo sitting on her bed.

YACHIYO: Okusan thinks of me as her friend. She confided in me about her husband. I, too, confided in her about Willie. How can she stay married to Takamura-san. He is such a rude and awful—

(Lights come up on Willie.)

WILLIE: Yamaguchi-san was beat up. Badly. All da workers' families getting kicked out of da camps. Babies, kids, living in da streets and da influenza going around like fire. Some of da older workers think maybe we should quit. Not Yamaguchi-san. *"Pau hana.* No go work. We on strike." *(Starts to leave, then stops)* Maybe it's better you stay there.

(Willie looks around furtively, then hurries away. Yachiyo seats herself on her bed. The Ochawan *sits next to her on her stand. Takamura arrives, weary, after a night on the town, bottle in hand. He sees something in her room, enters.)*

YACHIYO *(Scared)*: Takamura.
TAKAMURA *(Picking up the* Ochawan*)*: Where'd you get this?
YACHIYO *(Grabbing it back)*: Okusan gave it to me.
TAKAMURA: You don't know what you're holding, do you? Do you?
YACHIYO: It's an *Ochawan.* For Tea Ceremony.

TAKAMURA: No, no, it's much, much more Yachiyo. It's my blood. It's what gets me up each morning, lets me live. It's what makes me die each night after a long day of failure, knowing I will never be good enough to be his son. I gave it to her. It's my wedding gift to Sumiko. My father made it. *(Laughs and sits down next to her. Drinks from his bottle)* You remind me of someone. But then they all do now.

YACHIYO: How can you treat Okusan like this? Seeing that girl at the taxi-dance hall. Shame on you!

(Takamura stares at her, surprised at her fervor. He likes it.)

TAKAMURA: The woman inside awakens....Here. Why don't you drink with me. Come on, drink—

(Takamura puts his arm around Yachiyo and tries to make her drink from the bottle. Yachiyo pushes the bottle away and slaps him.)

YACHIYO *(Shaking)*: GET OUT!

(Silence. Takamura stares at Yachiyo. Then, slowly, he rises and goes to the door. Stops.)

TAKAMURA: What did she tell you? That she was the poor mis-understood wife? That I was cheating on her behind her back? I never lied to her. Right from the beginning she knew what I was. She knew exactly what she was getting. *(Pause)* She liked me. Why I shall never know. She became infatuated with me. Had to have me. Begged, cajoled her father until—ahh, the father. He was a shrewd, shrewd bastard. He cared little about anything but what he could buy and sell for a profit. And he could do that better than any man I've ever met. Have you down on your knees begging him to stick his hands into your pockets. And he could smell a man's weak spot a mile away. Profit, that's all he cared about. That is, except his daughter. His only child. That was his weak spot. And since his daughter wanted me, he made sure she got me. The old man offered me a proposition. I get a second chance to be the artist, to redeem myself in my family's eyes. In exchange, I marry his daughter and—ahh, here's the catch—I give up my name. *(Pause)* I don't know if I really cared one way or the other at the time. So you see, her father bought me for her. Like a pet dog. And she knew what I was. What she was getting. *(Pause. Unsure whether to reveal more)* We had an agreement. This one was between Sumiko and me. Her father didn't know. I told her I didn't love her. And that she must allow me my freedom. That I would be discreet and never bring her shame. This was my side of the bargain. She agreed. Maybe I am getting a bit careless of late—ever since the old bastard died. I guess you could say I've been celebrating. He'd like me drinking, though. That's the one thing we had in common. *(Silence. He drinks from his bottle)* You have a lover, don't you.

YACHIYO *(Hesitant)*: No.

TAKAMURA: You don't have to lie to me.

YACHIYO: I'm not lying to you.

TAKAMURA: A man like me can just smell it. We have a nose for it. You aren't so easy because your heart is full of some boy. Ahh, but if it should be distracted....Why don't you marry him? Raise a litter of babies.

(No response.)

TAKAMURA: Can't make up your mind, huh? Think maybe something better is out there.

YACHIYO: No.

TAKAMURA: Not necessarily a lover, but just something, some-thing...(*Pause*) I couldn't make up my mind once. She married someone else. I began to drink too much, gamble too much. Finally my father kicked me out. I should have killed myself. I think my father would have preferred that. Instead, I left for America. I wanted to forget, start all over. I couldn't even do that right. I gambled my money away on the boat coming over and got stuck here. But then a man without his real name doesn't exist anymore. Not really. I guess, in a sense my father got his wish, huh.

(*Takamura staggers out of her room.*)

YACHIYO (*Watching him leave*): Hiro...

(*Yachiyo notices he's left behind his* hachi-maki. *She picks it up, touches it. Places it next to her pillow along with the* Pikake *flowers and lays down staring at it. Lights fade to black. Lights up. It's Okusan calling to waken Yachiyo.*)

OKUSAN: Yachiyo? Yachiyo? Yachiyo, wake up...
YACHIYO: What is it?
OKUSAN (*Getting Yachiyo up and dressed*): We have to go get Hiro. He didn't come back tonight. I'm afraid all those pots he threw will be too hard in the morning to trim.... We have to make him come back tonight. He has to come back tonight or everything will be ruined.
YACHIYO: Why don't we just put wet towels on them—
OKUSAN: They're some of his best work yet. We have to save them, we must save them for him.... I already harnessed the horse to the carriage.

(*As she ushers Yachiyo out, Okusan notices Takamura's* hachi-maki *next to her pillow. Okusan follows Yachiyo and they seat themselves side by side in her horse-drawn carriage. Night. The moon. We hear night sounds. Ominous feel.)*

I saw a *hachi-maki* on your pillow. It looked like Takamura-san's. The one he lost.

YACHIYO *(Uncomfortable)*: I found it. I was going to return it to him.

(As they ride in silence, the world around them begins to transform. It grows dark, skewed—as if we could see the growing turmoil inside Okusan's mind reflected in the exterior world. Okusan abruptly continues her doll story.)

OKUSAN: She was so lonely. And though she loved him, he was not able to return the love. But she already carried his love within and could not release it. It grew inside her soul until she was filled with inconsolable grief. No one could help her. No one could save her...

(Long silence. Yachiyo wonders what's wrong.)

YACHIYO: Okusan?

OKUSAN: Until one day a young girl arrived. She befriended the woman. The pain inside subsided. The young girl made her feel happy again...

(Okusan notices where they are and pulls the reins to stop the carriage. The world returns to normal. We hear the muffled sounds of music and laughter. They both stare at the taxi-dance hall.)

He's in there. With his girlfriend. Some farm girl from Manila they painted up to look like a woman. And he pays five cents a dance to be with her. Five cents a dance.

(Yachiyo notices that Okusan doesn't move.)

YACHIYO: I can go in. Okusan? I can go in and get him.

(Okusan doesn't respond. Yachiyo gets out of the carriage and goes into the taxi-dance hall. Loud music is blaring and the room is bathed in a garish red hue. A couple whirls by dancing. Yachiyo stands there for a moment disoriented. She is both frightened of and drawn to the atmosphere of this world. Takamura is dancing with the young girl, played by Osugi. Yachiyo approaches him.)

Takamura-san? Takamura-san?

DANCE HALL GIRL *(Speaking in Tagalog, a Filipino dialect)*: *Lumayas ka!* He's all paid up!

(Takamura notices it's Yachiyo. Lets go of the other young woman.)

YACHIYO *(Talking over the music)*: Takamura-san, Okusan is waiting outside.

TAKAMURA: Dance with me.

DANCE HALL GIRL: *Puta!*

YACHIYO: Okusan's outside.

(Takamura grabs Yachiyo, pulling her to him. They begin to dance. Yachiyo is trying to politely get away but he holds her tightly. She finally relents and stumbles along with him. Okusan, wondering what has happened to Takamura and Yachiyo, enters. She sees them dancing together. Lighting change. Takamura and Yachiyo isolated in a pool of light. Sound dips.)

OKUSAN: But maybe the young girl was only pretending. Maybe she was deceitful and full of lies.

(Yachiyo and Takamura now dance smoothly. Yachiyo is uncomfortable but enjoying it. Okusan watches. Dim to darkness. Lights come up on Yachiyo.)

YACHIYO: It is now five months that I've been at the pottery. Takamura was pleased with the test tiles. I have—

(Lights come up on Takamura opening the small test kiln. He pulls out the test tiles and eagerly looks at them.)

—noticed a change in Takamura-san. In how he treats me. He no longer is so mean to me. Okusan, however, seems distant. During Tea Ceremony she has become very strict with me. When I want to talk with her she says—

(Okusan appears doing the Tea Ceremony. Her lines overlap Yachiyo's.)

OKUSAN: It is not correct form to make small talk about our personal lives...

YACHIYO: —"It is not correct form to make small talk about our personal lives," that it somehow, "breaks—

OKUSAN *(Overlapping)*: ...breaks the correct mood for the appreciation of the tea...

YACHIYO: —the correct mood for the appreciation of the tea." I miss talking to Okusan. Her behavior towards me is confusing. I noticed something. The tea. It no longer tastes quite so bitter.

(Okusan turns to watch Yachiyo. Lights on Okusan fade to black. Takamura and Yachiyo face off. They're both hot and thirsty. They've been building the kiln.)

TAKAMURA: The point of the *nobori-gama*, the climbing kiln, is that it re-uses the heat over and over. The heat used to raise the temperature in one chamber travels up to the next chamber and heats it up. And on and on. Instead of having seven separate kiln firings you have one extended firing, saving time, money and fuel. We have to check the angle of the kiln again.

YACHIYO: Didn't we just check it?

TAKAMURA: I'm not sure, I want to look at it again.

(Yachiyo dips her cup into the water bucket and drinks greedily, water spilling over the front of her clothes. Takamura laughs.)

YACHIYO *(Gasping for air)*: What?

TAKAMURA: It's dripping all over your clothes.

YACHIYO: I'm thirsty.

TAKAMURA: You drink like a dying horse.

(Yachiyo stops drinking.)

Drink, drink some more. I enjoy watching you.

YACHIYO: I'm crude, I know. Okusan keeps telling me that in Tea. I'm trying as hard as I can.

TAKAMURA: I like it. It reminds me of when I was young. When it's hot, you sweat. When you're thirsty, you drink. There's no need to overthink things, that muddies everything up. Too much thinking, too much logic makes the simplest things seem impossible. How far apart are we? Two feet? Half of two feet is what? One foot. Half of one foot is what? Half a foot. *(Moving his hand closer to Yachiyo's face)* Half of one-half is one-quarter. Then one-eighth. Then one-sixteenth, and on and on and we'd never touch. We'd always be a fraction of a distance away from each other, or so the men of science would like us to believe. . . . But for the Artist of course. . . *(He reaches out and touches her cheek)* The life of an artist. You live a life of immeasurable suffering. But there are some rewards—you get to experience poverty and public ridicule, too. *(Pause)* Here, let me show you something in the *nobori-gama*. I noticed it while we were working. See, a bird is building her nest in the first chamber.

YACHIYO *(Moving away)*: I'll clean it out—

TAKAMURA: No, no, let it build. It'll be long gone before we have to fire. Besides, I love the sound of baby birds chirping. Like little children singing to us. It'll make our work easier when we're loading all the pots into the chambers. Keep track of the nest for us. If need be we can always move it.

YACHIYO *(Going back to work)*: Hiro?

TAKAMURA: Yes?

(She takes out a worn sheet of paper from her pocket and hands it to Takamura. It's the composite picture of Yachiyo's Montgomery Ward ensemble.)

What is this?

YACHIYO: It's what I'm going to look like someday. When I grow up.

TAKAMURA: What did you do, cut this out?

YACHIYO: Un-huh. Out of the Montgomery Ward Catalogue. I make them up. I cut out different pieces of clothing and then paste them together. It's a game I play with myself and sometimes with my friend Osugi. What we'd like to look like one day. *(Beat)* Only for me it's not a game.

(Pause. Takamura doesn't know what to say. Yachiyo takes it from his hands and folds it up.)

I thought you might like to see it. That's all. I just wanted to show you.

(Yachiyo goes back to working. Takamura watches her. Takamura dims to darkness.)

I feel a little guilty. I did not think about—

(Lights come up on Okusan. Yachiyo dims to darkness. During Okusan's following monologue, Takamura is lit holding a dress.)

OKUSAN: Dear Mr. William Higa. This is a rather embarrassing situation, but I feel I must write to you. Your fiancée, Yachiyo Matsumoto—who as you know works with my husband and myself—has. . . . How do I say this—she has developed a romantic interest in my husband. He, of course, is embarrassed by the whole situation.

(Okusan freezes. Takamura fades to black. Lights come up on Willie, very agitated, bleeding. We hear the plantation siren and the commotion of men being beaten.)

WILLIE: Dear Yachiyo. Da company's goons attack us with horses and guns—we had only sticks to fight back with. Da head of da Pilipino Federation now siding with da company bosses—he sold his union out. But Yamaguchi-san says we have to all stick together. "No barriers of nationality, race or color." *(Pause)* How come you don't write?

(Lights on Willie dim. Okusan comes out of her freeze.)

OKUSAN: —before she does something to embarrass all of us.

(Mama is lit in a pool of light next to Okusan.)

As I do not have your address Mr. Higa, I am sending this care of Yachiyo's mother and father. I am sure we can trust them not to take advantage of the situation and that this unfortunate circumstance will remain a secret just between the two of us.

(Lights come up on Yachiyo holding a dress. Continuation of Yachiyo's prior scene.)

YACHIYO: I feel a little guilty. I did not think about Willie all day.
OKUSAN: Signed, very sincerely yours, Mrs. Hiro Takamura.

(Okusan hands the letter to Mama. Okusan exits. Mama stares at the letter, looks up towards Yachiyo who is holding the dress. Willie appears and Mama hands him the letter. As Willie takes the letter he looks from Mama to Yachiyo, then exits. Yachiyo, with her mother's eyes on her, withdraws still clutching the dress. Mama is silent for a moment. Then, as Mama dims to darkness, lights rise on Yachiyo, Takamura and Okusan. They are doing the Tea Ceremony. It is Yachiyo's regular lesson; however, Okusan has insisted that Takamura participate. Okusan whips the tea up and offers a cup to Takamura who drinks following all the correct movements. He is obviously trained in this.)

Yachiyo? Why don't you try on your new dress?

(Yachiyo is silent.)

Hiro says the color becomes you.
YACHIYO *(Embarrassed)*: I cannot accept it. I told Takamura-san.
OKUSAN: But why not?
TAKAMURA *(To Okusan)*: It's just a dress. I saw it in the store and I thought she might like it.
OKUSAN: I think it is wonderful that you think of Yachiyo.
YACHIYO: I asked Takamura-san to take it back.
OKUSAN: No, no, that is unthinkable. You must wear it for me. Please? *(Pause)* After all. It's the one you wanted, isn't it, Yachiyo?

(Yachiyo is silent. She takes out Yachiyo's Ochawan.)

Let's use this one. The one I gave you. *(She glances at Taka-mura, then begins to prepare Yachiyo's tea, whipping it to a froth)* I was talking to Mrs. Lee next door and she said a girl from your camp was found unconscious. She had taken ant poison. Her parents found her just in time. A Shimokawa girl. Do you know her? Maybe we should get you a hat. To go with your dress. What do you think Hiro? *(Back to Yachiyo)* Would you like that?

(Yachiyo turns the cup three times and drinks. Wipes the lip and sets the cup down.)

How do you find the flavor now, Yachiyo. Still too bitter?

(Pause.)

YACHIYO: I'm starting to like the taste.

OKUSAN: I was once told *Chanoyu* tea could never be appreci-ated by someone of a pure nature. The flavor, the bitterness would overwhelm the innocence, the purity of the person's palate. Only when one has walked through the, how do I say this politely, the human excrement of life, is one capa-ble of understanding, appreciating, finding pleasure in the complexity of its *ningen no aji*, its human flavor. *(Beat)* I'm glad you're beginning to "like" the taste.

(As Okusan continues with the Tea Ceremony, Takamura and Yachiyo glance at each other. Dim to darkness. Mama is lit in a pool of light. Willie appears holding the now-opened letter. His arm is bandaged.)

WILLIE: Matsumoto-san?

MAMA: I read it. I'm sorry. *(Pause)* Do you think it's true? What Mrs. Takamura said?

WILLIE: I'm going there. To Waimea. To see Yachiyo. *(He exits)*

MAMA *(Calling after)*: I don't believe it! Mrs. Takamura lied!...

(Dim to darkness. Then, Yachiyo is lit in a pool of light in the upstage area. She is putting on the dress Takamura bought her. Her curiosity piqued, in the privacy of her room she has finally decided to actually try it on. Further downstage, Takamura appears in the shadows silently watching Yachiyo dress. Yachiyo senses something and turns, covering herself. Takamura-san ducks back into the shadows, still watching. Yachiyo goes back to putting the dress on. We almost get the sense that Yachiyo knows who is watching and that she enjoys the sensation. As Yachiyo starts to adjust the dress and comb her hair, Takamura hears something and turns to leave. Oku-san appears and they exchange looks as he exits. Okusan sees Yachiyo in the pool of light adjusting the dress. Yachiyo glances back, still assuming it's Takamura. However, unbeknownst to Yachiyo, it is Okusan in the shadows watching her. Okusan glances back towards the exiting Takamura. Fade to black. Then, lights come up again on Yachiyo. Okusan enters. Yachiyo is embarrassed at being caught wearing the dress.)

OKUSAN: I think the hat would go well with your new dress. Don't you think so?

(Yachiyo is silent. Okusan approaches her, admires the dress, touches it.)

Do you enjoy sleeping with my husband?
YACHIYO: What?
OKUSAN: Or, maybe a shawl. Would you prefer a shawl? Hiro gave you this dress. Then I shall give—
YACHIYO *(Overlapping)*: Okusan, what are you saying?
OKUSAN: —you a shawl.

(Pause.)

I said, Do you enjoy sleeping with Takamura-san?

YACHIYO: Please, Okusan, I am not sleeping.... I'm not doing anything with Takamura-san. He just gave me this dress, that's all.

OKUSAN: I could tell your parents. You know that of course. Such an ungrateful.... I trusted you. No one knows the things that I have told you. No one.

YACHIYO: Okusan...

OKUSAN: No. A hat. Yes. I think a hat would be better.

(Okusan exits, leaving Yachiyo in her room. Willie approaches Okusan as she leaves.)

WILLIE: Mrs. Takamura?

(Pause. Okusan is not sure who he is.)

OKUSAN *(Realizing)*: Willie Higa?

WILLIE: Where's Yachiyo?

(Okusan gestures towards Yachiyo's room, where Yachiyo remains in half light. Willie starts to turn, then stops. Pulls out the letter.)

OKUSAN: From Yachiyo's parents? From you?

WILLIE *(Handing the letter to Okusan)*: It's da letter you sent. Dey asked me to give it back.

(Willie turns and approaches Yachiyo. Okusan watches for a beat, then exits.)

Yachiyo.

YACHIYO *(Surprised)*: Willie...

(Yachiyo stares for a beat.)

What are you doing here?

WILLIE: I came into Waimea with—

YACHIYO *(Overlapping)*: It's good to see you.

WILLIE: —my brother. *(Pause)* I rode with him in his wagon. We rode all night.

YACHIYO *(Noticing)*: What happened?

WILLIE: Just a scratch. During da fighting.

(Beat.)

YACHIYO: Did your brother have business here? Is that why he came to Waimea?

WILLIE: No.

(Awkward pause.)

I'm supposed to be at work. Drank a whole bottle of *shoyu*, da soy sauce made my blood pressure shoot up through da roof, my whole body, like it was crawling with ants. Fool da plantation doctor good.

(Willie moves forward and they awkwardly embrace. Willie remembers some Okinawan food that he's brought and gives it to her.)

From my mother, some *andagi*, the one you like—she made it for you special. *(He glances around the room)* Dis where you live?

YACHIYO: Un-huh.

WILLIE: You look a kinda skinny. Bag of bones, yeah. Dey feeding you good?

YACHIYO: I get plenty to eat. They treat me very well.

WILLIE: Good, good, 'cause your Mama and Papa are worried. You look good, though. I like da dress. Did you buy it here?

(Yachiyo doesn't respond.)

YACHIYO: It seems funny to see you standing there. In this place.
WILLIE: What do you mean?
YACHIYO: When I see you, it's like I'm trying to remember me.
WILLIE: A lot of things have happened at da plantation. I haven't heard from you so I don't know if you got—
YACHIYO *(Overlapping)*: I've been very busy...
WILLIE: —my letters or not.

(Pause. During Willie's monologue, Yachiyo moves away and watches as lights rise gradually on Takamura, who is asleep. Next to him, sleeping, is the young woman from the dance hall. Takamura wakes up.)

Dey got rid of Fagundez. We got a new *luna* now. Guess who da new foreman is? Yamaguchi. Finally, a *Nihonjin luna*—da first Japanese foreman. Dey give us everything we ask for after we give in. I'm kind of important now, a big shot. Not really a big shot, like a *luna* or anything. But since I know Yamaguchi-san, da older men, dey treat me differently now.

(As Takamura gets up, the young woman from the dance hall tries to get him to stay in bed.)

DANCE HALL GIRL: Hiro? Hiro-chan? Come back to sleep. Hiro?

(Takamura looks back, turns away in disgust and stumbles towards Yachiyo and Willie. Lighting change. Yachiyo, Takamura and Willie are lit.)

TAKAMURA: Who's this?

YACHIYO: This is my friend from Mana. Willie Higa.

(Takamura stares at him.)

TAKAMURA: So you're the one.

YACHIYO: This is Takamura-san.

(Silence.)

Willie and his brother had some business in Waimea. He decided to come visit.

TAKAMURA: He knows who I am. *(Pause)* Sumiko wrote you, didn't she?

(Beat.)

YACHIYO: What did she write you Willie? Willie?

WILLIE *(To Takamura)*: She told you?

(Pause. Takamura watches Willie.)

TAKAMURA: No. *(Getting in Willie's face)* Did she write that Yachiyo is getting quite formidable in the Tea Ceremony? Or that, that, Yachiyo is quite accomplished at mixing clays now and prepping the studio. Did she write that I'm not paying enough attention to her or, or that I gave Yachiyo this new dress. Did she write you about that?—

YACHIYO: Takamura-san, please…

TAKAMURA: *(Backing Willie up)* —What's this? A bandage for the little cane field worker trying to bring the big bosses to their knees. You can't change things, little cane field worker, didn't you know that? Someone will always be above you, bigger than you, better than you Okinawa boy, putting you in your place, telling you what to do, slapping you around, beating you with a stick—

(Willie wields Takamura around and slams him against the wall.)

WILLIE: SHUT UP! SHUT UP! SHUT UP!!!
YACHIYO: Willie, let him go! Willie!…

(The force of the banging causes the Ochawan *to fall and shatter. Willie stops. Takamura notices the broken* Ochawan. *Stares at it. Then, bends down and picks up a piece.)*

WILLIE: Who the hell do you think you are anyway? Huh? Who the hell do you think you are?

(Takamura picks up a shard and stares at it for a beat. Then digs it into his palm. Stares at the blood.)

TAKAMURA: I don't know. I don't know anymore…

(Takamura stumbles away. Lights come up on Mama.)

MAMA *(To Willie)*: Willie?
WILLIE *(To Mama)*: Everything's fine Matsumoto-san. Yachiyo's all right. Nothing's going on.

(Pause.)

MAMA: Good.

(Silence. Willie and Mama stare at each other. Willie turns to look at Yachiyo. Then Willie exits. Mama looks at Yachiyo, then dims to darkness. Yachiyo bends down and begins to pick up the pieces of the broken Ochawan. *Takamura is at the water's edge. Bluish pond lights. He stares at himself in the water. Yachiyo enters and approaches him cautiously. She sits*

down next to him. She offers him a folded cloth with the pieces of the Ochawan.*)*

YACHIYO: Maybe we can piece it together. Re-glaze it. Fire it again.

(He stares at it, then looks away. Yachiyo places it down beside him.)

I watched you here. One time. You couldn't see me. You were drunk.

(Takamura is silent.)

The eggs are beginning to hatch. The nest in the kiln? You can hear the babies calling for their mother to feed them. You were right. It's a nice sound. It helps the work.

(Pause.)

I sent him home. Willie.

(Silence.)

TAKAMURA: We'll be firing soon. We may have to move the nest.

(She takes a cloth and pats Takamura's bleeding wound. At first he pulls away but eventually relents. She has her face close to his and is watching him. She works in silence for a beat. She leans forward and kisses him. He gently pushes her away.)

YACHIYO: I thought.... I don't understand Takamura-san. *(Beat)* I know you've been watching me. At night. When I go to bed. I know it's you. It doesn't matter. Hiro? I don't mind...

(Takamura doesn't respond.)

I thought this is what you wanted. I should have gone back with Willie. He asked me to, you know. He begged me to go back home with him.

TAKAMURA *(Quietly, barely audible)*: I can't. I just can't Yachiyo.

YACHIYO: What? Takamura-san, what?

TAKAMURA: I can't do this.

YACHIYO: Hiro.

TAKAMURA: You don't want this kind of thing. You don't, Yachiyo.

YACHIYO: Okusan's accused me of sleeping with you. She did, she thinks we're lovers. Now, Willie believes it, too. Why shouldn't we, then? Huh? Why shouldn't we?

(Takamura is silent.)

TAKAMURA: Go home. Back to Willie. Back to your old life Yachiyo.

YACHIYO: I don't want to go back. I can't go back.

(Yachiyo takes a piece of the broken Ochawan. *She digs it into the palm of her hand. Blood appears.)*

Okusan was right. About the tea. I like it now. I like it a lot.

(She reaches out and places her bleeding hand on his cut hand. Yachiyo moves forward and kisses Takamura. He embraces her. The water gradually washes over them and becomes blood red. A rippling sound score, like wind over water. As they embrace, the lights on them fade to half and lights rise on Okusan. Upstage of her are two dolls. The dolls mirror the embrace and movements of Yachiyo and Takamura. As Okusan watches the dolls, Yachiyo and Takamura fade to black.)

OKUSAN *(Watching the dolls)*: They do not move to my wishes. I cannot make the world inside my head be the world out there. I must make it move to my wishes. I must make sense of this...

(Okusan dims to darkness. Lights up on Yachiyo watching the two dolls make love.)

YACHIYO: His skin was not smooth like Willie's. It was both coarse and smooth. His face, his hands were rough. But under his arm, the back side of his thigh, his skin was like a little boy's. I would run my fingers over those places and he would laugh because it tickled him and his joy would fill me with childish pleasure and I would feel like a little girl gorging on overripe mango. But when I touched his stomach he would grow quiet and the laughter would become thick with musty, sweet odors. And I could feel my own breath growing heavy, the air inside me a prickly heat and I would want his sex, now hard in my hand, to carry me on its swollen current, drowning beneath dark wet fingers.

(Dolls fade to black.)

When I look in the mirror, I cannot see myself the way I used to. Just me, my face looking back at me. My own thoughts, my own feelings. I can only see myself through his eyes now. How does he see this face? How do I look to him? Am I pretty enough? I cannot tell where my face ends and his eyes begin.

(Lights come up on Takamura. He moves in behind her.)

And when he touches me, I want his hands to grow into my body, sending roots deep into my flesh. Each touch a new root pushing into the deepest part of me, taking hold, growing into a tangle around the wound that is my heart so we would always be together, nothing could ever separate us.

(Takamura withdraws.)

I am in pain and yet it is so pleasurable. At times I cannot think, I cannot breathe. And to be apart from him for even an instant feels as if time has stopped and I am only waiting, waiting. Until he is there again and I can breathe. I wish it would stop, this feeling. I wish it would never end.

(Lights come up on Takamura at the small test kiln, hurriedly opening it and taking out the pots. They are still hot and he tosses one after another aside as they are not good. Takamura finds one and stares at it, then takes out a red cloth and wipes the pot off. He holds it up and looks at it with satisfaction.)

TAKAMURA: Yachiyo, look!

(As Yachiyo is about to move towards Takamura, Okusan is lit. Takamura sees Okusan. He wraps the pot in the red cloth and reluctantly hands it to her. Okusan stares at the pot, then at Yachiyo and Takamura.)

OKUSAN: I'm beginning to understand.

(Takamura and Okusan fade to black. Yachiyo moves into another light. Loud, rhythmic sound. The feeling is fast-paced, hurried with no sentimentality. Mama and Papa are lit. Willie is lit playing Hana. He slaps the cards down and makes loud exclamatory sounds. Osugi is lit doing housework.)

MAMA: Yachiyo?

PAPA: Yachiyo?

OSUGI: Yachiyo?

WILLIE: *Chikusho.* [Dammit.]

MAMA: Yachiyo.

PAPA: I started writing poems again.

MAMA: We haven't heard from you.

PAPA: Mama doesn't know.

OSUGI: The Shimokawa girl.

MAMA: How are you?

PAPA: They aren't half-bad.

OSUGI: She go so far.

MAMA: Papa and I were talking.

PAPA: You stay there. Study—

MAMA *(Overlapping)*: Maybe you should come home...

PAPA: —Tea, flower arrangement...

OSUGI: Cannot come back.

MAMA: Yachiyo...

WILLIE: Yamaguchi...

PAPA: Yachiyo...

WILLIE: He's siding...

OSUGI: Yachiyo...

WILLIE: ...with the bosses...

(Pause.)

MAMA: Are you "friendly" with Mr. Takamura?

WILLIE: *CHIKUSHO!!!*

(Sound punctuation. They all move hurriedly past Yachiyo as she attempts to talk to them; then they exit, leaving her alone. Takamura enters, distracted.)

YACHIYO: Hiro?

TAKAMURA: Not now, not now—we have work to do. Is the clay prepared? I'm going to try some new designs...

(They work in silence. Yachiyo watches Takamura. He notices her staring.)

Stop doing that.

YACHIYO: What?

TAKAMURA: You're looking at me. Staring at me.

YACHIYO *(Aside)*: I can't help myself. I find myself watching him all the time. It's as if I have no control over myself. And the more he tells me not to look, the more I must watch him, as if my eyes had their own hunger...

(They work in silence.)

Do you think about going back to Japan?

(No response.)

I wouldn't mind going there.

(No response.)

Your pottery has become so good. Okusan said so. You could be famous. More famous than your father. Maybe he would take you back if you showed him some of your pots. You could return home. I would go back with you Hiro—

TAKAMURA: My father is dead.

YACHIYO: I don't understand. You said he was still alive—

TAKAMURA: He's dead and so am I. Now leave me alone, I need to work.

(Lights come up on Okusan doing the Tea Ceremony. Yachiyo moves over and joins her.)

OKUSAN: You turn it two times.

YACHIYO *(Seating herself)*: What?

OKUSAN: You turn it two times, not three.

(Yachiyo turns the cup two times, then drinks in several sips of the thick, astringent tea. Then, silence.)

Takamura-san is working so hard these days.

YACHIYO: He is not nice to me.

OKUSAN: When he works, he is happy. I have you to thank for that. Don't I.

YACHIYO: What do you mean?

OKUSAN: When Takamura-san is happy, I am happy. And he is happy now. *(Holds pot up. Admires it)* He made it in the smaller test kiln. It is his best piece yet. You cannot tell, can you? It is quite beautiful.

YACHIYO: Pots. That's all he cares about. This damn pottery. Day and night, night and day. *(Pause)* Why is he ignoring me now? What did I do?

(Okusan doesn't respond, continues looking at the pot.)

I'm sick of this pottery. And this damn Tea Ceremony, too.

(Yachiyo exits angrily. Okusan is alone.)

OKUSAN: You did everything you could be expected to do. But now. Now he needs something more.

(Okusan holds the pot and quietly smiles to herself. Dim to darkness. Lights come up on Papa.)

PAPA: Yachiyo. Mama finally put her foot down. She made me go to Hamada's store to talk about our...money problem. You know how I hate that kind of thing, having to argue with people. It wasn't so bad. Hamada was actually under-standing of our situation with me not working right now. When I happened to mention I was writing poetry he asked if I could write letters for him. I said, "What, Hamada-san you can write." He said, "No, for the workers. Love letters."

(A pool of light comes up on Mama working. Yachiyo is lit.)

YACHIYO: Mama?

(Mama stops and looks towards Yachiyo. Continuation of the earlier scene.)

Yes. I am friendly with Mr. Takamura.

PAPA: *Sensei*—that's what the workers call me. "*Sensei*, tell her I've got muscles as hard as stone, can work a twenty-four-hour day and that we won't have to live down below, but high on the hill in a huge house above the *lunas*, or even the plantation boss! Make her want me so badly, she'll swim here!"...I write letters for the workers who want wives back in Japan. They send pictures and exchange letters. And they pay me for my services. Not a lot, Hamada gets a percentage. But I'm working. Mama is happy. Mama?

YACHIYO: Mama? *(Pause)* I love him.

MAMA: Yachiyo...

(Fade to black. Lights come up on Takamura and Okusan.)

TAKAMURA *(Upset)*: I don't know, I don't know—my father was right.

OKUSAN: Hiro...

TAKAMURA: What if the clays can't hold this type of heat, they didn't even work in the test kiln—

OKUSAN: It worked, it worked, you made your best piece—

TAKAMURA: But everything else cracked—was it the clay, the heat, the kiln, I'm not even sure what I did to make that one pot? And the *nobori-gama* is totally different. Much more complicated. What if the angle is all wrong? We've wasted all these months building a useless kiln, your father's money all used up on this—

OKUSAN *(Overlapping)*: Hiro! Hiro, listen to me...

TAKAMURA: —goddamn kiln that won't even fire...

(Pause.)

OKUSAN: It's all right, don't worry. It will work. I know you can do it.

TAKAMURA: I keep seeing his face watching me, my father's face. I become paralyzed. I can't do it, I just can't do it...

(Takamura breaks down. Okusan comforts him like a small boy.)

OKUSAN: He's not here. It's not important what he thinks. You can do it. I will help you...

(Lights on Takamura and Okusan dim to half. Lights come up on Yachiyo. Yachiyo sees Okusan comforting Takamura like a small, crying child. She is confused to see Takamura acting so uncharacteristically. And seeking comfort with Okusan. Yachiyo approaches them.)

YACHIYO: Hiro? Hiro, what's the matter? Hiro?

OKUSAN *(Waving her away)*: Yachiyo...

YACHIYO *(Persisting)*: Hiro? It's me, Yachiyo. Are you all right? Hiro?

TAKAMURA *(Angrily)*: Get out! Get out of here!

(Yachiyo, confused, withdraws. Dim to darkness on Okusan comforting Takamura. Yachiyo is lit by the kiln. She is listening to the sound of the mother bird feeding the babies.)

YACHIYO *(Upset)*: I love the sound. The mother comes and goes bringing food to the babies. I think we will be firing the kiln soon so we will have to move the nest.

(Lights come up on Mama. Continuation of the earlier sequence.)

MAMA: You, "what"? You "love him"?
YACHIYO: Mama...

(Pause.)

MAMA: Your Papa, his family was so against our marriage. I didn't come from a good family, wasn't trained in the arts the way young girls are supposed to be. Papa didn't care. He married me anyway. I went to live with his family. They all looked down their noses at me. Especially the sisters, oh, his two older sisters. . . . Papa could tell how much I hated being treated like that. Finally, he decided—and he made up his own mind—that we would come here and start all over. He came first, then soon after called me over. Left his family, the life he knew, so I could be happy. He did that for me. *(Beat)* You "love him..." He's married Yachiyo. What's this man going to do for you? *(Pause)* Are you sleeping with him? Yachiyo?
YACHIYO: I want to come home. Can I come home? Mama?

(Pause.)

MAMA: If you want to.

(Yachiyo understands Mama's implicit message. As Papa enters, Yachiyo dims to half. During the reading of Papa's letter, Yachiyo pulls out a sprig of Pikake *flowers and inhales its scent.)*

PAPA: Since I started doing all his business correspondence we can have anything we want at the store now. I'm practically handling all his negotiations—a whole new line of things from Japan and from San Francisco. Yachiyo? If you want you can come home now. Hamada said we can even order the Singer sewing machine... *(He moves to Mama)* Did you hear what I said? Are you still upset with me? We paid everything off—

MAMA: Do you still think about going back? To Japan?

PAPA: What?

MAMA: Do you regret coming here?

PAPA: I'm working again, it's more suited to what I can do. I'm good at it. And we don't have to ask my sisters for any more help.

MAMA: Hisao?

(Pause.)

PAPA: Yes. I do regret it.

(Papa and Mama fade to black. Yachiyo goes to the water and kneels, watching her reflection.)

YACHIYO: Sometimes I would awaken at night, go to the mirror and stare at myself. In that world of shadows and dream, I would recreate... *(Pause, thinking)* Recreate...

(The male and female dolls are lit making love.)

And he loved her very deeply... *(She watches the dolls for a moment)* Just like that. Yes, perfect.

(The dolls dim to darkness. Yachiyo gets up and takes a cloth from between her legs and washes it in the water. There is no blood. Yachiyo frantically washes the cloth in hopes that it will show a trace of blood.)

I missed my period again.

(Lights come up on Takamura working. Okusan, in half light, moves to the large climbing kiln. She has the two dolls with her. She places them into the kiln, lights a match and stares at it. Fade to black. Yachiyo approaches Takamura.)

Hiro.

TAKAMURA: Not now, Yachiyo.

YACHIYO: Hiro, I have to—

TAKAMURA: Prepare some mortar so we can seal up the doors on the upper chambers—

YACHIYO: Takamura! *(Pause)* You have to stop this. Stop ignoring me. You have to start paying attention to me. Like you used to.

TAKAMURA: I don't have time for this now, there're so many things I have to—

YACHIYO: I'm pregnant.

(Silence. Takamura goes back to work.)

TAKAMURA: I've got work to do. I have to ready everything.

YACHIYO: What are you doing, did you hear what I said?

TAKAMURA: What do you want me to do? What? I'm married, Yachiyo.

YACHIYO: I don't care, I don't care—let's go away. Let's run away together. Osugi's parents did it. Her mother was a picture bride and didn't like her real father so she ran off with Mr. Chong.

TAKAMURA: I can't do that, I just can't do that.

YACHIYO: Why not, why can't you Hiro?

TAKAMURA: Yachiyo, look at me. Look at me. I'm not a young man.

YACHIYO: We can be happy, we'll be so happy together...

TAKAMURA: I ran away once before. I just can't do that anymore.

YACHIYO: We can go to the Mainland or back to Japan and you can build a pottery, start all over. We can have the baby, get married there and no one will have to know—

TAKAMURA: Yachiyo! Yachiyo!

(Silence.)

I'm not strong enough. I'm weak. That's always been my problem. My father knew it. He always knew it. Maybe that's why I hate him so much. This is my last chance. I need this. I need to be strong enough this time.

YACHIYO: So you need Okusan?

TAKAMURA: Go back to Willie. He'll marry you.

(The kiln explodes with flames.)

My god, she lit the kiln. She started the firing...

(Takamura runs to the kiln where Okusan stands watching.)

YACHIYO: The nest, the nest...

(As the kiln burns, a flaming bird soars out of it into the night air. Yachiyo stares in horror as the mother bird, engulfed in flames, thrashes wildly about. We hear the kiln roar, the frantic fluttering of wings and the screeching of tiny birds.)

OKUSAN *(Looking at the kiln)*: Look, look, what a glorious sight!

YACHIYO: The mother bird…

OKUSAN: You have to grow up now, Hiro…

YACHIYO: …her wings, whole body…

OKUSAN: …or you lose everything.

YACHIYO: …on fire…

OKUSAN: You have no time to be scared of your father. *(Looking at the flames)* This is my gift to you.

(Takamura stares at Okusan for a beat. Then he runs up and pulls a plug out of a kiln portal opening and looks at the flame.)

TAKAMURA: The wood we stocked in earlier seems to be allowing the fire to burn correctly. The pull seems a little strong up the center. We need some smaller, hotter burning wood for the edges—it'll help pull the flame to the sides. Sumiko, more wood! Yachiyo make the mortar so we can shut the sixth and seventh chambers!

(As Yachiyo watches, Okusan turns and stares at her. For a moment Yachiyo returns the look. Then, Yachiyo slowly moves away. The kiln flames die and the scene fades to black on Takamura and Okusan. Takamura glances back at Yachiyo. For a beat, Takamura and Yachiyo are lit in pools of light, staring at each other. Takamura fades to black.)

YACHIYO: And he loved her very deeply. He loved her very deeply.

(A night sky. A big moon.)

YACHIYO: I walked all night. Through the reddish soil. By early morning I had reached Mana. *(She notices something, reaches down and picks up a sprig of* Pikake *flowers)* Pikake.

(Inhales and comes to a realization) No dreams. I am awake. Awake and nothing else. *(She lets the flowers fall to the ground)*

(Lights come up on Willie returning from a night of drinking and gambling.)

WILLIE: What are you doing here?

YACHIYO: I've come back home. I missed you.

WILLIE: Things have been busy here. That's why I haven't written. They started a new union. Japanese and Pilipinos together. Yamaguchi and I have to keep an eye on them. For the company bosses. *(Beat)* I'm making good money now...

(Pause.)

YACHIYO: Willie? Let's get married.

(Willie doesn't respond.)

Willie? Please...

(Instead of responding, Willie moves to embrace her. He is rough, forcing himself on her. Yachiyo pushes him away.)

WILLIE: You let him, didn't you? *(Pause)* All right. I'll marry you.

(Yachiyo doesn't respond.)

I said I'll marry you.

(Silence.)

YACHIYO: *(Quietly)* No…

(Willie withdraws.)

…to preserve her family's honor. To save face for herself and her parents. Because there was nothing else to do…

(Lights rise to half on Mama and Papa upstage sleeping. Yachiyo stares at a bluish watery pool of lights that appears before her. The lights begin to move over her.)

YACHIYO: Polihale Beach. The sun is just beginning to rise. The water. It's like a mirror. I will see the world from the other side. Through her eyes. I enter the water and swim out far beyond the breaking waves. My arms ache and my legs already weary from walking all night begin to cramp. But I continue to push out until the shore appears a distant shadow. *(Noticing)* The sun… *(She watches the sun breaking the horizon)* And then I dive. Deep beneath the surface.

(Lights and sound.)

My face feeling the cold lick of salt and wetness. Deeper and deeper, straining my arms, kicking with my legs. Forcing myself to go farther and farther down. The water is bone-chilling, blackness everywhere, my air running out. Still I push myself down, down—I must go so far. So far that I cannot come back.

(Pause. Sound cue builds as Yachiyo realizes she has no air left. She panics, changes her mind. Overhead a light appears representing the surface above.)

No air, no air left, I'm choking, suffocating—I have to get back to the surface, I need to breathe, I need to breathe so badly I can feel my face about to explode. I see the sunlight entering from above. Cutting through the water like long transparent knives. I want them to cut me open, peel me out of my skin so whatever is me, whatever is wanting, needing to breathe so badly can get out...

(She struggles fiercely. Blackout. Deep, echoey, crash. Mama and Papa, sleeping in half light, begin to stir.)

PAPA *(Waking up)*: Yachiyo? Yachiyo?
MAMA: What is it Papa?
PAPA: Yachiyo, is that you? Yachiyo...

(Yachiyo is lit. Light goes from warm to brighter and brighter during the following speech.)

YACHIYO: Lately I feel so many things. Sometimes I feel I am going to burst. It is not a bad feeling, but it makes me confused. I'm always expecting something to happen. Something new. Something good.

(The light on Yachiyo becomes tightly focused, a very intense white light. Then, very slow fade to half on Yachiyo. As lights dim on Yachiyo, they rise on Takamura at the kiln pulling the bricks out of a chamber door. Okusan is lit in a pool of half light, watching him.)

TAKAMURA: After what I have done to Yachiyo, surely the Heavens would not reward me...

(As he takes out the pots, one after the other, he stares at them.)

TAKAMURA: My god. ... They're beautiful...

(Takamura embraces a pot and bows his head in despair.

Okusan holds up a pot and stares at it. She smiles and begins to hum a lullaby to herself. Yachiyo, who was in half light, pulses for a beat to brightness, a cascade of white petals drifting down around her. She pauses, her expression changes, as if something troubling has intruded into her thoughts. Lights quickly fade to black. Super titles appear:

DEDICATED

TO THE MEMORY OF

YACHIYO GOTANDA

1902-1919

Dissolve to the portrait of the real-life Yachiyo.)

END OF PLAY